To Joel, Hannah, and Emma—
my sun, moon, and stars.

*And it took cutting back
the prettiest parts of myself
to finally realize that this shell
does not define me.*

*For I am so much more
than the flesh and bone
that case the beautiful tragedies
of my heart and mind.*
~Becca Lee~

DUCK AND COVER

The sun sits in a brilliant blue sky, making the snow sparkle. To the west, cows and hay bales speckle the rolling hills right to the foothills. Snowy Rocky Mountains rise in the distance. I used to want to live right in the middle of those mountains. Not anymore. A shiver comes over me, and not just because of the cold breeze that whips the air.

Simon and I walk down the long driveway toward the township road. My boots squeak on the packed snow where Dad's truck plowed a track on his way to work early this morning.

"I thought you were my best friend," I say.

"I *am* your best friend, Abby. What could be worse than taking the school bus and facing everyone right off the bat?" His bushy brown hair and eyelashes are tinged with white frost.

"Nothing is worse!" The scar on my thigh rubs against my near-frozen jeans. I stomp my foot, which does nothing to stop the irritation. Just when everyone thought spring had arrived, the weather turned icy. March in southwestern Alberta always keeps you guessing.

"All the gawking, pointing, and sniggering will fizzle out in the twenty minutes it takes to get to school. Then you're done," says Simon. "I'm doing you a big favor. Besides, all the major players are on this bus—Serena, Briar, Grace, Liam..."

I was really hoping to avoid Liam. Praying that he changed schools or went on the student exchange to Spain like he'd talked about or was abducted by aliens. Nice aliens, not the ones that dissect human bodies and extract organs.

I thank every deity ever dreamed up that Mason drives his beat-up truck to school and no longer takes the bus. But I won't be able to avoid him for long. Please, please, please don't let him be in my drama class. My stomach suddenly feels like I drank a pitcher of sulfuric acid.

I dig in my jacket pocket for the figurine my grandma gave me while I was in the hospital. A small wooden carving of a bear standing upright on its hind legs, arms outstretched, head thrown back. I take off my glove and rub the smooth surface with my thumb and then hold it tightly.

The school bus heads down the road toward us. I breathe deeply, creating an icy fog and pull my scarf over my face. I try to quell the shakiness in my body. My heart beats a heavy-metal drum solo. I grab Simon's arm, something to hold me up. As the bus pulls to a stop, I see a row of faces in the frosted windows, including Liam's, peering out at me—the freak show.

The door swooshes open. I push Simon's tall lanky body ahead of me.

"Simon, to what do I owe this pleasure? Jeep in the shop?" Kelly has been the same bus driver on our route since we started at Rocky View High in grade nine.

"Just couldn't stay away from you any longer, Kelly."

Her face opens into a big smile and she slaps her knee. The thick roll around her belly jiggles when she laughs. "Hey, Abby. Welcome back," she says.

"Thanks for the card you sent me," I say quietly as I climb the steps and pull the hood of my jacket over my head as far as it will go. But it doesn't cover enough of my face. I hide behind Simon as he makes his way down the aisle. Out of the corner of my good eye I can see people's reactions—going wide-eyed like they've just seen a bad accident, doing double takes, craning to see more of me under my hood, talking behind their hands. I feel like puking.

"Hey, girlfriend," Serena says to me in a cheerful way that sounds as fake as her thick, curled eyelashes look. "What's up?"

Briar, Serena's wannabe clone and my replacement, sits with her and waves lazily at me with her bright orange nails, barely taking her eyes off her phone. The disaster that is my face is old news to Briar. She already closely scrutinized me when Serena brought her over to my house last fall soon after I got out of the hospital. The whole twenty-two minutes and forty-two seconds they were over. Briar's mouth gaped, her eyes opened as wide as anatomically possible, and her eyebrows raised so high I thought they'd disappear into her hairline.

Grace is in the seat across the aisle.

"Glad you're back, Abbs." Grace stands, her black corkscrew curls stuffed under her red hat. She searches my face with her dark brown eyes in a warm, gentle way and gives me a big hug.

"Thanks."

I spot Liam sitting by himself and our eyes meet. I pull the scarf higher over my face. My heart pounds even harder. He quickly shuts his eyes, leans his mop of blond hair against the window, and listens to music I can hear coming through his earbuds. Probably Kongos or The Killers.

Simon leads me to the bench at the very back of the bus and sits beside Jackson, his fellow computer geek. They bonded at nerd camp at the University of Calgary last summer.

"Hey, Abby." Jackson looks everywhere but right at me. His cheeks are round and red. He still has braces on his teeth.

"Hi." I sit.

I keep holding tightly to the wooden bear. As Simon and Jackson natter on about programming languages, all I can think about is how much I dread walking through the school doors.

***

Being on display in front of the whole school is far worse than the bus ride. I feel naked as crowds of students in the hallway, heading for class, jostle me. I try to be invisible under my hat and scarf, but a group of pesky grade nine boys points at me. They don't even try to hide their disgust. People I've known since elementary school stare. When they finally clue in by mentally rearranging the puzzle pieces of my face, they offer feeble greetings.

Mason and Dax are laughing and joking with a group of guys. In true Mason style, just for sport, he trips a poor unsuspecting grade nine boy, who falls flat on his face. Books and papers fly across the floor. His buddies laugh even louder. I have to stay as far away as possible from Mason for the next few months until school ends. Keeping my head down, I weave away through the swarm.

Near the school office, the glass case still displays photographs of last spring's drama performance, *Saint Joan,* by George Bernard Shaw. There I stand, center stage as Joan of Arc, my army of French compatriots behind me. My hand raised, beseeching Commander Dunois to lead the forces against the English. That night was pure magic. As soon as I was on that stage, the rest of the world fell away. Sounds weird, but I truly felt that night I embodied Joan of Arc. I swear I could even hear the voices of Saint Margaret and Saint Catherine, the angels who were sent by God to guide Joan on her mission. My lines flowed out of me as if I never had to memorize or rehearse them. I study another close-up shot of me. In spite of with the harsh shadows of the theater lights, my face looks normal, even pretty. I want to sit down right here in the main hallway and bawl my eyes out.

I'm supposed to be heading for biology class. Instead I take a detour behind the stage of the auditorium. I try the door to the prop room. Locked. I walk around to the door at the other side of the stage and find the costume room open. Dresses, pants, shirts, flouncy blouses, ties, hats, shoes, and bolts of different kinds of fabric are stuffed on shelves.

I look in the large oval mirror hanging on the wall: the two sides of my forehead sewn in a permanently puzzled look, the left side of my face sunken like a landslide, my crooked mouth that won't close properly. I try on a smile, like I've done about a million times, but my mouth is all wonky and refuses to cooperate. One angry red scar starts on my scalp, continues down my forehead, and slices too close to my right eye, forming a thick scar over my eyelid. I can barely see out of this eye. I've been told to be thankful I didn't lose it altogether. The scar continues right down my cheek. I take off my hat and look at the side of my head where the reddish-brown hair that used to be one of my better features is growing back in patches. I touch the little islands of hair on the back of my head. I take off my jacket and lift up my T-shirt. Three gashes: one on my left breast and two above, where the grizzly almost tore open my chest. I turn and look in the mirror at my back where there's scarring from a skin graft.

I sink to the floor and breathe in the musty smell. Tears well in my eyes and spill down my cheeks. Sobs start to shake my whole body.

I make sure the halls are empty before I dump my jacket in my locker. My eyes and cheeks are still red from crying, and I'm now about thirty minutes late for biology class. I pull my hat down and position my scarf as high as I can over my face. I open the door. The class is suddenly quiet; even Mr. Jessop stops talking mid-sentence. Everyone stares at me. I find an empty desk at the back where I won't be on display and sit down. I scan the class. Serena sits beside Liam, and I mean her desk is *right* beside his. She puts her hand on his arm, leans very close, and whispers something in his ear. He smiles weakly. I can see him blush from way over here. I wonder if she said something about me, or maybe that's my paranoia coming out to play. Just in case, I tug my scarf as high as it will go without covering my whole face. Now that I'm deformed and therefore "undateable," Serena's moved right in. It's poetic: the two people who dumped me have come together.

"Serena, could you please tell Abby what we've been discussing," says Mr. Jessop.

"Umm...well," Serena flips through her notebook, "we've been talking about different kinds of...sacca...sac-cah-arides." She's always been very brainy in the sciences. Liam's obviously a distraction for her in this class.

"Good attempt, Serena. Liam, what can you fill in for Abby?"

Liam looks straight ahead at Mr. Jessop. "Saccharides are the unit structure of carbohydrates. We've been discussing the differences among monosaccharides, disaccharides, and polysaccharides."

"Thank you for that, Liam." Jessop heads for my desk. "Abby, you'll find the information starting on page sixty-four of the textbook, but you've got some catching up to do. Come see me if you need help." Jessop hands me an assignment I did from home so I wouldn't fall too far behind this semester. Fifty-six percent. Shit. Guess I'm really behind. I flip through my assignment to see where I went wrong. Pretty much everywhere.

Jessop goes back to the front of the class. "Okay folks, for the last few minutes of class, pair up and go over the assignment that's due Friday. Liam, I'd like you to pair up with Abby."

Best and worst bio students. I can tell from here that Liam is rolling his eyes. Serena turns around and shoots me an annoyed look.

Liam drags himself to where I'm sitting as if an invisible force field is holding him back. The desk scrapes on the floor as he turns it around to face me, but he only looks down at the paper in front of him.

"It's pretty straightforward," he says. I notice his fingernails have been chewed right down. "Examples of monosaccharides are glucose, fructose, galactose, and—"

"Why haven't you returned my texts and phone calls?" I burst out. I want to punch him and kiss him at the same time. "It's been over seven months." I'm loud. Others look over at us, including Serena. Including Mr. Jessop.

Liam finally looks at me with his hazel eyes, blankly studies my face. What's he thinking? On his forehead, a blond lock of hair curls in the shape of a question mark. My body tenses, braces for a verbal blow. He shifts his eyes, stares at a corner of the ceiling. I can almost see the pulleys and cranks turning in his brain, searching for the right words. Then he looks at me again with his mouth open.

"It's just…I…," he garbles, then grabs the assignment, walks to his desk, and stuffs his papers and books into his backpack. Suddenly, inside my head, it's like a stereo turned to max volume. I hear Liam's frantic screams. "Help me. Someone help!" Like a crazy person, I put my hands over my ears, trying to drown out the sound that only I can hear. As I watch Liam leave the class, my heart sinks right down into my Doc Martens.

Before next class, I head into the washroom and lock myself in a stall. I don't even have to pee. I just sit on the toilet seat. I need peace and quiet to calm the furious noise blasting my brain. The washroom door swings open.

"If I were her, I'd never show *that* face around school—ever." I recognize Briar's voice.

"Geez, Briar," Grace says, "give it a rest."

"She's got a point," says Serena. I peer through a crack in the stall. "Abby must know everyone's talking about her. I mean, how couldn't they?"

I lift my feet off the floor and gently press my boots against the door, in case they look under. I hear the clicks of makeup cases and tubes of lipstick. Last year, Serena, Grace, and I would meet here between almost every class to touch up our makeup. And to gossip. Sometimes to say mean things about other girls.

Serena continues, "She could have finished high school online. Why would she put herself through this?" She runs a comb through her long blond hair.

My heart thumps so hard I can feel it throbbing in my ears.

"Well, I think she's brave," says Grace. I look through the other crack and see her leaning against the wall.

"That's maybe one word to describe her," says Briar, and she and Serena giggle.

"Why shouldn't Abby come back to school and graduate with her friends?" Grace asks.

"Ah yes, grad," says Serena as she twirls her hair into a bun and knots it on the top of her head.

"Has Liam asked you yet?" Briar asks Serena.

"Not yet, but I'm going to make sure he does."

I gasp, covering my mouth to mask the sound.

"Have you even thought that maybe he has other grad plans?" Grace says. She knows Liam and I planned to go to grad together, and Liam always keeps his word. Even if he might not want to. Like when he promised his cousin he'd go to a BMX race with him the same weekend our hiking group planned a sweet backpacking trip to the Whaleback Trail in Yoho National Park. He stayed home and went with Ryan like he'd promised. And the time there was a party in Sundre, but Liam had already promised his mom he'd work the evening shift at Java Junction, the café she owns.

"Other plans? You mean Abby?! You're kidding, right?" Briar says.

"Why not Abby?" Grace asks.

"Seems a bit obvious to me." Serena puckers her lips at the mirror and grabs her turquoise designer purse.

"Ditto that," says Briar, who takes Serena's place at the mirror and mimics her exact same pucker.

"I can't believe you two." I see a flash of black curls as Grace heads for the door. It whooshes as it opens.

"By the way, when are we going shopping for grad dresses?" Serena asks. "There are some cool new stores in Kensington I want to check out."

They leave.

And I feel like a boulder is crushing my chest.

SCHULTZY

I walk into the drama room and catch a glimpse of myself in the mirror that covers one whole wall. For a brief hallucinatory moment I see my old face. I scan the room. Guess who's in my drama class: Mason. Great. Just great. He and Dax sit across the circle of chairs and stare at me disgustedly, reminding me of what my face has become. Mason says something behind his hand and they both laugh. Tali, Zoe, and Tammy are chatting. I find a free chair beside Carter and Leon.

"If it isn't the drama queen herself," Leon says. He's been jokingly calling me that since I won the lead role in last year's play. He played one of the male leads—Robert de Baudricourt.

"Hey, Abby," Carter says.

"Hey, you two," I say. Both sneak peeks at my face, trying not to be too conspicuous. I can only imagine how shocking it is.

"Abby, what do you get when you cross a dyslexic, an insomniac, and an agnostic?" asks Leon.

"No idea," I say.

"Someone who lies awake at night wondering if there is a dog."

"Ha ha, very funny," I say.

Carter jumps in. "What happened to the cow that jumped over the barbwire fence?"

"Dunno," I say.

"Udder destruction." When Carter laughs at his own joke, he bends right over as if he's going to summersault off his chair. "Leon and I are starting an online joke bank. Got anything for us?"

Mason hasn't stopped staring at me. My brain jumps to an image of Venom from Spider-Man, with jagged patches for eyes, hundreds of razor-sharp teeth, and a long slithery tongue spitting poisonous slime at me from across the room.

"Clean or dirty joke?" I ask.

Leon and Carter look at each other. "Something in between," Leon says.

"In the spirit of winter weather in springtime, what's the difference between a snowman and a snowwoman?" I say.

They shrug.

"Snowballs."

"Ha! Nice one." Carter types the joke into his phone.

Mr. Owen, Rocky View High's drama teacher, hurries into the classroom. "Listen up, everyone." He slaps some files and notebooks onto his desk. Owen rides everyone's ass hard and doesn't take any shit. I'm pretty sure he doesn't even like kids. But he's the one who made me fall in love with drama my first year of high school. Way before he took a chance and cast me as Joan of Arc. After the performance, in his gruff roundabout way, he told me I didn't suck too badly.

"As most of you already know, drama week is a few short months away. For the night of the Graduate Drama Showcase, I'm giving one group of grade tens the opportunity to perform a short play before all of you take the stage. For you, the graduating class, instead of performing an ensemble play like we've done for the past few years during drama week, you will have a choice. You will write and perform either a monologue or a one-act play. Three to five minutes max for the monologues and eight to ten minutes max for the plays. Don't be fooled into thinking shorter means easier because it's not. Monologue folks will be on their own, but play people will choose a partner. You'll both write, act, and direct each other in rehearsals." I see a few people pair up. No one looks in my direction. Guess I'm on my own.

Owen runs his fingers through his ginger hair then strokes his beard, like he often does when he lectures. "Sky's the limit in terms of subject matter. However, you're ready to graduate from high school. A milestone. I want evocative. I want soulful. I want heart-wrenching. What have you learned about life thus far? What is important to you? What do you care deeply about? What event has profoundly changed your life?" Owen looks right at me. I look down at my feet. "This is your chance to tell the world. And it damn well better be interesting and engaging. Questions?"

"Can it be a comedy?" Carter, the king of improv, asks.

"Why not? But you'd better make me laugh until I cry and then make me laugh again. Remember that very thin line between comedy and tragedy. Anyone else?"

"When do we perform?" Zoe asks. Her dirty blond hair is cut short except for a long, thin ponytail dyed bright purple. She has a small tattoo of a red rose on her upper right arm.

"You will first present your plays to the class for critiques. Then you will perform for your fellow students and the community during drama week."

"Is that before or after grad?" asks Tali.

"A few days before. Don't worry, Tali, you'll still have plenty of time to spruce up for grad." Tali smiles, her cheeks turn a rosy red. I imagine her in a seafoam-green dress draped over her lily-white skin. Her frizzy red hair nicely flat-ironed. A super-hot grad date (obviously not anyone who goes to this school). Serena, Grace, and I used to say nasty things about Tali's chubby body, her thick glasses, or something she wore. Even though we always said these things behind Tali's back, we were mean. Really mean. The shame feels like a heavy rock sitting in my stomach.

"I will need you to email me first drafts by the end of next week or sooner," Owen continues. "Back to you for a rewrite. Back to me for another read. Back to you for as many drafts as it takes. Rehearsals will begin as soon as I think your monologue or play is worthy. Therefore, the more work you do up front on your writing, the more time you'll have to rehearse. *Capisce?*"

A monologue. That means I'll be onstage. Alone. I can't hide behind makeup, costumes, or my fellow actors. *Shit!*

"Let's start class today with an improv," Owen says. "Mason, you're up first. Choose someone to join you."

Mason looks right at me. I stare at my feet, imagine myself melting into a miserable puddle on the floor.

"I choose Abby."

No, no, no, no, no...

Mason stands and struts to the front of the class.

"Abby?" Owen gives me a questioning look, wondering if I'm up for this my first day back in drama class. I'm not, but everyone's looking at me. Waiting. I'm glued to my chair. How can I get out of this? Owen moves to the back of the room where he always watches students perform. Too late to say no.

My knees are wobbly as I slowly get up and stand beside Mason. His musky boy smell is strong. He's not only beefy, but he towers over me—I think he's gotten even taller in the last several months while I haven't been around.

"Prompt please?" Owen looks around the class.

"Breaking up," Dax shouts, louder than "trapped in an elevator" and "a conversation in purgatory."

No, no, no, no, no…

Mason puts his head down and covers his face with his hand, shakes as if he's crying. There's a stubble of black hair on his shaved head.

"I'm sorry," I say and put my hand on his shoulder. He shrugs me off and glares at me.

"Sorry? Are you effing kidding? After what you did to me?" Mason says. Suddenly, I have a strong sense that we've time-traveled back to a year and a half ago in the school parking lot, sitting in his truck.

"Well, it's great that you have a hot new girlfriend, right?" I say brightly, trying to change direction.

"And unlike *you*, I'm sure she won't cheat on me with another guy," Mason says.

I look around the class. By the expressions on everyone's face, they know this isn't just an improv. This is reliving a past nightmare that I wanted erased from everyone's memory. Especially Mason's. Especially mine.

"Stay in role, Abby," Owen says. He hasn't a clue what went on between Mason and me. Owen is not one of those warm, fuzzy teachers.

I look into Mason's gray eyes. "Look, I know I was an A-1 jerk. But everything turned out for the best, didn't it?" Again, I try to sound really cheery. He shakes his head and looks away from me. His fists are clenched as if he's ready to throw a punch. Like the time he punched a hole in his rec-room wall when I told him he was suffocating me and I needed space. While calling me a frigid bitch, he ran his bloody knuckles under cold water and wrapped them in gauze. I shiver at the memory. "Okay. What can I do to make it up to you?" Now I'm going off script; I never did ask Mason this.

He turns to me. "There's nothing you can do to make it right. But don't worry, you'll pay for it."

"Okay, thank you." Owen cuts it short. The tension is palpable. "Applause for our actors. Who's up next?"

Mason goes back to his seat and high-fives Dax. I'm pretty sure when Mason said I'll pay for it, he wasn't acting. But so much time has passed. Why does he still feel he needs revenge? Especially now, with my deformed face. It's not as if he would ever want me back as his girlfriend. It feels like a knife has been plunged into my chest.

Schultzy wants to meet with me during phys ed, my last class of the day. Great timing because I wasn't looking forward to changing into my gym strip and showing off even more of my scarred body to Serena, Briar, and Grace. Mrs. Schultz, the school counselor everyone calls Schultzy—even to her face—is the students' favorite of all the school staff. Even though her off-white nylons rub together making a scratchy Velcro sound when she walks, and she wears various shades of gray polyester skirts and blazers with "comfortable" shoes, she's still the coolest teacher at Rocky View High. When Simon's mom went all *Eat Pray Love* over a year ago and took off for an ashram in India, he spent many a day curled up on Schultzy's comfy office couch. I wish I had known her when I was ten, when my mom died of cancer.

I knock on her open office door.

"Well, look what the cat dragged in," she says. I have a quick flash of the bear's jaws around my head, dragging me down the path. A shiver shoots through my body. Schultzy takes off her glasses, lets them dangle on the silver chain around her neck. "How are you?"

"Okay, I guess." I'm suddenly weak and quivery.

She eyes me carefully. "If I were in your shoes, I'd be scared to death coming back to school."

"That too."

"If anyone gives you trouble, come and see me, you hear?"

As if. I'm already low on friends and nobody likes a snitch.

"Still in pain?" she asks.

"My leg still gives me trouble." I touch the left side of my face. "But here, I just have a constant ache."

"I have to tell you, Abby, I'm so impressed with how you've handled this trauma. It would be a tall order for anybody to live through, but you've come this far with such maturity and grace."

"Thanks." But neither she nor anyone else for that matter has any idea what's really going on with me. I have my own kind of crazy that I hide from everyone.

"Have a seat." Schultzy puts her glasses back on and rummages through files on her desk until she finds mine. She flips through it. "Considering you missed all of last semester and several weeks of this one, you're at least, well, holding your own. Let's see your marks in the online courses you completed in the fall. Social studies and English marks are good, math mark is okay." She peers up at me over her glasses. "What are you taking this semester?"

"Biology—only because I need a science credit—phys ed, and drama."

Schultzy pushes her glasses up on her nose as she flips through my file. "Pretty light term you've got."

"I finished all my required courses online. The Internet is a beautiful thing."

"Lots going on in the drama department this term."

"I'm not exactly lead-role material anymore." The words come out shaky, and I sound pitiful.

"Have you applied to any college or university theater-arts programs yet?"

I shake my head. "Plans have changed."

"Abby, you have heaps of talent. Don't let anything get in the way of your dream of becoming an actor. And I mean *anything.*" She stares at me for an uncomfortably long time. "Promise me."

"Okay," I say, but it's a promise I can't keep. When I first saw myself in the mirror after the bandages were unraveled from my face, I knew that unless I was auditioning for *The Elephant Man*, all my dreams for the future had come crashing down.

GRIZZLY DIARIES

I knew this day would suck, but I had no idea how bad it was going to get," I say to Simon as we walk down my driveway. I tell Simon about the bathroom incident with Serena, Briar, and Grace, but I don't tell him about Mason. I so want to obliterate that incident from every brain cell.

"Whatever you do, don't get caught back in the Sticky Hive," Simon says. "Besides, Queen Bee Serena is clearly moving in on your boyfriend."

"Liam is no longer my boyfriend. He's fair game." My heart sinks as I say those words. A dark ridge of clouds forms a Chinook arch at the edge of the mountains. It's made the air much warmer. I unwrap my scarf and unzip my jacket. My bad leg aches as we trudge through the sloppy snow.

"Did he actually break up with you? Formally, I mean?" asks Simon.

"Didn't have to. We've barely spoken since I got out of the hospital. You saw how he acted on the bus."

"Liam's a good guy, Abby." Simon splashes in a puddle like a preschooler. "Maybe he just needs some time to, you know, get—"

"Get what? Used to my face? Come on, Simon, look at me. I've had about a hundred counseling sessions over the past several months, and I've cried buckets over the undeniable fact that my dating days are over at the tender age of seventeen. Unless maybe I meet a guy who's blind or who looks as ugly as me."

"You're going to have more surgeries."

"Seven surgeries so far and my face still sends young children screaming to their mothers' arms. I'm coming to terms with it. Or at least I'm trying to. Well, not really." My voice is shaky and I feel the tears welling.

Simon gets very uncomfortable around raw emotion. He walks quickly to reach the path he takes home through the neighbor's property.

"See you tomorrow, Abby."

"See you." I wipe a tear that has spilled down my cheek.

I walk toward the over 100-year-old farmhouse that's been in my dad's family for generations. One of the original homesteads in the area. My ancestors used to look out at cattle and horses grazing on the wide-open prairie. The wraparound porch now looks out onto enormous homes sitting on an acre or two, including Simon's. This used to be a farming and ranching community. Now residents vacate Springbank every morning and head about a half-hour east into downtown Calgary for work. My dad included. When he can find work, that is.

Dad and Mom were going to renovate our house from top to bottom. They even had an architect draw up plans. But the reno plans died with Mom. Now paint peels off the trim, the front steps have wiggly boards, and the porch sags.

My cell phone bloops a text: *Home from school, bean?*

Almost, I reply.

FaceTime?

In a few

K

***

I sit propped up with pillows on my bed, my computer in my lap.

"Did you get my other text this morning? Sorry if it was at dawn. My math class is so bloody early," Jeannie says, looking like a cubist painting through the screen.

"No worries. Slept right through it." My sister is the only one I feel truly comfortable with on FaceTime.

I hear the *click-click-click* of Ruby's nails in the hallway. Ruby's our black-lab-collie-husky-golden-retriever-and-who-knows-what-else mutt. She hears Jeannie's voice and jumps on my bed, starting to whine. "Ruby. Hello my sweet, adorable canine," Jeannie says. "Is she getting gray hair?"

"A little," I say and hug Ruby's head. "That's what happens when you're almost sixty years old in human years."

"How did it go today?"

I shrug. "I made it. Just barely."

"Must have been so ridiculously hard."

"I'm sure it'll get easier. Then again, maybe it won't," I say.

"It will. Mainly because my sister happens to be the most incredibly together, brave, amazing person on the entire planet."

"What? Not the galaxy?"

"Okay, the whole universe," Jeannie says. "By the way, now that you're back at school, have you thought about a grad dress?"

"Gawd, you sound like the Hive."

"The what?"

"Never mind. And no, I haven't thought about a grad dress. Besides, I'm big-time struggling with bio, so I don't know if I'll even be able to graduate this year."

"I so wish I was there to help you," Jeannie says.

"Yeah, why did you get all the science and math genes? Speaking of, how's university? Meeting more cute guys this term?"

"As a matter of fact, yes. Caleb, from my Chem 110 class, asked me out to a concert at the Commodore. Some band from Austin, Texas."

"You hate music."

"I don't hate it, it's just not totally my thing. And if I have to endure it with a gorgeous guy, oh well." Jeannie tucks some blond curls behind an ear. "How about you? Did you finally get a chance to talk to Liam today?"

I shake my head. "He's avoiding me like I've got Ebola or some other deadly disease."

"I don't understand him. He came to see you in the hospital almost every day."

"Only when I had bandages covering my face and head, and I was so drugged up I was either sleeping or hallucinating from the morphine. When my bandages came off—poof! He disappeared."

"Well, screw him."

"Not anymore." I can't help but smile.

"You're so bad." Jeannie checks a text on her cell phone.

"Caleb, I presume?"

"No, Baljinder, my physics lab partner. Wants to study."

"I should let you go."

"I miss you like crazy, Bean. Grandma booked me a flight home for Easter. Yay! Only a few weeks away. Can't wait to get out of Vancouver. So much rain. I miss snow and blue skies and sunshine and you and Dad and Ruby, of course."

"Miss you too, J, even more than dryer lint."

"I miss you more than soggy, limp nacho chips," she says.

"I miss you more than falling into a mud puddle."

Jeannie laughs. "Unfortunately, I know all about mud puddles these days. FaceTime next week? Ciao, ciao." Jeannie blows me a kiss and disconnects.

**

No one knows about my disturbing obsession. And I mean no one.

I take my notebook out of the bottom drawer of my bedside table. Loose papers I've printed off spill out the sides. I read over the first page as always. Part of my macabre ritual.

Grizzly Bears

Facts:
- The grizzly is a North American subspecies of the brown bear, but not all brown bears are grizzlies.
- The Latin name for grizzly is Ursus arctos horribilis (a.k.a. horrible northern bear).
- Fur is generally brown, but can be white-tipped or grizzled, hence the name.
- Can move as fast as 30 miles an hour.

- Solitary creatures—except moms travel with cubs, and males gather together for fish feasts when salmon spawn.
- They dig dens for winter hibernation, often in the side of hills.
- Females give birth during the winter, offspring are often twins.
- Grizzly bears are top-of-the-food-chain predators, but most of their diet is made up of nuts, berries, fruit, leaves, and roots.
- Bears eat other animals, from rodents to moose.
- GRIZZLY BEARS CAN BE DANGEROUS TO HUMANS, PARTICULARLY IF HUMANS COME BETWEEN A MOTHER AND HER CUBS.

I read over the last line about a hundred times, until my eyes can't focus anymore. It's a strange kind of self-torture. I started this bizarre research a few months ago in the hope that filling my brain with facts while I'm awake would chase away my nightmares about the attack. Sometimes it even works.

Second step in the ritual, I look up the "Weekly Bear Report" on the Parks Canada website. On my large topographical map of Alberta and British Columbia hanging on my bedroom wall, I stick in colorful pushpins where grizzly bears have been sighted—mostly locations in Banff, Jasper, and Yoho national parks—right in the wiggly, wavy lines where the Rocky Mountains are. Dad thinks I'm marking out hikes I've either been on or hope to go on.

Next, I read articles online about grizzly bears and take notes. Then I look through photos of bears and bloody bodies attacked by grizzlies.

Finally, I search YouTube for video clips or documentaries about grizzlies or grizzly bear attacks, or review ones I've already seen dozens of times. Today, I find a new one with a narrator who has an English accent. In the documentary, the bears are given names like Woofy, Teddy, and Tuffy. The narrator's voice is so soft and soothing it sounds like he's reading a bedtime story as he talks about how males sometimes kill and eat their young. I'm pissed off by this documentary, making grizzlies seem like stuffed animals you can play with. Male bears fight for the right to mate with whatever female happens to be around, the documentary says. Barney, an old male grizzly, mounts and humps Tuffy, an alpha female. A bigger and younger male, Sebastian, comes along and growls and scraps with Barney. Out with Barney and in with Sebastian.

I flip to a blank page in my notebook and write down:

- Males eat their young.
- Males fight over females in order to mate.

For something different, I watch YouTube videos about grizzly bear mating behavior. Turns out, grizzly porn is not that exciting.

***

"Capital of Bulgaria," I say, then fork a last piece of chicken and stuff it into my mouth.

Dad thinks for a moment while he chews. His green eyes dart around looking for the answer. "Sofia," he finally says.

Dinnertime has been painfully quiet since Jeannie left for Vancouver last fall to go to the University of British Columbia. If I hadn't started this game to fill the air, Dad and I would have nothing to say to each other. And I mean nothing.

Dad's turn. "Capital of Australia."

"Too easy. Canberra," I say as I gather empty bowls and plates. "How about El Salvador?"

"Speaking of too easy, San Salvador." Dad scoops up the remaining clump of mashed potatoes on his plate. "Capital of New Zealand."

"Auckland, of course."

"Ah, got you." Dad points his fork at me.

"What?"

"Wellington."

"You're joking."

"Nope."

I check the globe on a side table and spin it to find New Zealand. "Oh man. Why didn't I know that?" I take the plates and bowls to the kitchen counter and load the dishwasher while Dad clears the rest of the table.

"School was okay?" Dad asks. I begged him to let me finish high school online, but he was the one who told me I couldn't hide at home with the covers over my head forever and insisted I go back to Rocky View High. But I think he really just wanted me out of the house. Especially on the days when he's out of work.

"Yeah, sure. School was fine." I squirt dish soap into a pan and start scrubbing.

***

I sit on my bed with my laptop. I hit "Save" on the bio assignment. I haven't gone on social media much since I ended up in the hospital. Too gut-wrenching to see all my friends moving on with their lives— partying, skiing, rock climbing, playing, hiking. Looking beautiful. But when I really want to torment myself, I creep everyone I know.

Simon's Facebook timeline first. Geek gadgets. Geek toys. Geek apps. Everything geek. Snoozefest. Why are we best friends?

Serena was always pretty, but in the last eight months, while I haven't been around, she's become drop-dead gorgeous. Every square inch of her.

Grace's timeline is full of adorable animal videos: a raccoon hugging a cat, a puppy licking the face of a hedgehog, penguins sliding on their bellies into the icy ocean. I go back to June of last year. Grace posted a photo of the two of us with big toothy smiles. *#BFF #PrayforAbby Everyone pray for one of my best friends, Abby, who is fighting for her life in the Foothills Hospital. Please share.* Serena shared Grace's post about me.

Grace came to see me in the hospital a few days after I was admitted. I was seriously drugged up, but I'll never forget the horrified look when she saw me, head and body wrapped like a bloody mummy. She dashed out of the room crying, probably barfed in the hallway. She and Serena called, texted, and visited me at home a few times after I got out of the hospital last summer, but the air between us was all scratchy. In the fall we stayed in touch, but they always had an excuse why we couldn't get together. Volleyball practice. Homework. Family dinners. Too tired or too hungover from a party. The three of us have been friends since eighth grade. It's painfully obvious I don't fit in with them anymore.

Mason. Nothing's changed. He's still all about violent video games. *Resident Evil, Mortal Kombat, Call of Duty, Grand Theft Auto. Naughty Bear?* What?

Liam. Still hasn't posted anything since last June. I check now and again, trying to figure out why he's incommunicado. Taken a vow of computer abstinence? Secret girlfriend? A fatal disease? The last photos he posted are shots of me in my climbing gear and ropes, hanging off the side of a mountain. Matt and Lisa, our climbing friends, are seen higher up the rock face.

Liam and I first got to know each other in grade ten, through Rocky View High's Outdoor Club. About once a month, Ms. Fanning, the outdoor ed teacher, would drive a van-load of us to the mountains and take us hiking. When our grade eleven hiking buddies—Thomas, Sarah, and Jarret—got their drivers' licenses, we ditched the club. Instead, a group of us would head out on weekends to go backpacking, hiking, backcountry skiing, and rock climbing.

One weekend, just after Liam got his driver's license, everyone bailed on a three-day backpacking trip to the Rockwall Trail. Everyone except Liam and me. I'm sure our parents wouldn't have been too impressed to hear it was just the two of us, but we never told them. After a kick-ass day of hiking, we sat around the fire roasting marshmallows till they caught fire, telling jokes, and laughing our asses off. We slept in our own tents that night, but the burning wood in the fire pit wasn't the only thing throwing off smoldering heat. The next morning we left our tents and packs and climbed up a scree slope. Never in my whole life will I forget that day. When we got to the top of the slope, we looked all around us—360 degrees of sunny, clear blue skies and snow-capped peaks. On top of the world. We were so awestruck we didn't say a word for about fifteen minutes. Then Liam held my hand. We sat on a rock and started to cry at the incredible beauty all around us. That night we slept in the same tent. It was too crowded in the sleeping bag to do much except kiss and make out a bit. Besides, condoms were not on our laminated backpacking list.

This was the first time I cheated on Mason. But it wasn't the last.

I quickly scroll through photos of the day that would change my life: Thomas, Jarret, and I in the parking lot adjusting our packs; Sarah making a funny face at the camera as we start off on the trail;

pheromones in all directions just to toy with unsuspecting schlubs like me?" Simon opens the door to the parking lot, and we walk to the sparkling new Jeep his dad bought for him for his eighteenth birthday.

"Was I, you know, as plastic as them?" Even as I say the words I know the answer.

"Uh, yeah!" Simon gives me a can-you-really-be-that-clueless look. "The only thing that saved our friendship is our history and our shared love of foreign films and decadent flavors of ice cream. And you were outdoorsy, which at least kept you somewhat grounded. But, boy, could you ever flip the bitch switch." Simon points his fob at the Jeep to unlock the doors.

Simon is right, and it makes me feel even worse than I already do. "Grace is outdoorsy," I say as I climb into the passenger seat.

"Used to be. The Queen Bee is not, so Grace stepped up her side-kick game this year—in a big way." Simon starts the Jeep.

I haven't heard Grace talk about snowboarding this winter or any hikes planned for the summer, and there's no evidence on Facebook or Instagram. But then again, what do I know?

***

I flip through a fashion magazine at Dr. Van der Meer's Calgary office. Images of models looking all beautiful and perfect. Good marketing ploy for a plastic surgeon's office. I put the magazine down and look over at Dad flipping through *Golf* magazine, a sport he's never tried but sometimes watches on TV. Two middle-aged women sitting across from us look like they've been seriously beaten up, with facelift bruising under their eyes and dark purple lines down their faces. One woman tries to hide her black eyes by wearing sunglasses. Inside. Not cool. And I can tell she's staring at me behind her shades. Also not cool. A younger woman, slim and fit, reads *Hello* magazine. I don't think those are her real boobs—too big, high, and perky for someone her size. I pick up a brochure from the magazine table. *Facing It: Supporting people with facial differences.* Dr. Van der Meer talked to me about this group last fall, but that was when I refused to leave the house, even to go to a meeting with people whose faces might be as scarred as mine. I toss a brochure into my purse.

Finally the receptionist calls my name and leads us to the exam room.

I sit on the table while Dr. Van der Meer inspects every inch of my face, as closely as I inspect hers. She has deep wrinkles at the corners of her eyes and two lines in her cheeks around her mouth. Laugh lines.

"Have you ever had plastic surgery?" I ask. Her face looks like a woman her age should look, but maybe she had some belly fat removed or something.

"Abby…," Dad says. Deferential to the medical profession, he thinks patients should be seen and not heard.

Dr. Van der Meer chuckles. "No, I haven't."

"Why did you become a plastic surgeon?" I ask.

"When my older brother was ten, he got cancer of the jaw, which, after several operations, disfigured his face. I wanted to help people like Jeff. People like you."

I have a feeling she makes most of her cash from facelifts, tummy tucks, and boob jobs, but I keep my mouth shut.

She touches the left side of my face. "How has it been feeling?"

"Okay, but it aches sometimes. Well, most of the time."

"Any fever, bouts of severe pain?"

"Not really."

"If anything changes, call my office and I'll get you in right away."

"When's the next surgery?" Dad asks.

"You're pleased with how you're healing. But I'd like to hold off a bit longer. Maybe schedule something for after Abby graduates." She turns to me. "We can work the surgery around your plans. Have you applied to college or university for the fall?"

I shake my head. "After June, I'll have nothing but time." No university, no work, no boyfriend, no life.

"OK then, I'll have my office set the surgery for mid-July."

"What will this surgery entail?" Dad asks all the important questions.

"I want to build Abby a new cheekbone."

"How are you going to do that?" I ask. I've heard her talk about this before, but I remain skeptical.

"I'll be shaving bone from one of your ribs and reconstructing your cheek. Then flaps of skin will be taken from your chest wall, thigh, or buttocks to cover the area."

Dad shakes his head, incredulous. "The wonders of modern medicine."

"You'd be surprised how successful this surgery has been. My brother is a great example."

I look at myself in the mirror hanging on the wall. I've already had seven surgeries, and I can't help but wonder if I'll ever look even close to normal.

✳✳✳

"You're wrong," I say, reading from my phone. "Wikipedia says the Caspian Sea is often regarded as the world's largest lake, but it contains an oceanic basin, rather than being entirely over continental crust. Whatever that means." On the drive home, we're stuck in traffic on Bow Trail, so Dad and I play our geography game.

"It's still regarded as the world's largest lake."

"Nice try."

"Which is the largest of the Great Lakes? And no surfing the web for the answer," Dad says. He pulls the truck forward until we're once again at a standstill.

"Easy-peasy—Lake Superior. The name tells it all."

"But did you know that it contains more water than the other four Great Lakes combined?"

"How do you know all this stuff? You need a life."

Dad looks out the side window, away from me. I've hit a nerve and it feels like an invisible curtain drops between us.

"Dad, what are your plans, you know, if or when I finally leave home one day?"

He waits for a long while, then shrugs his shoulders. "Only thinking day to day. How to keep a roof over our heads and food on the table."

I pause, muster up some courage. "You just seem so sad and lonely."

He shrugs again. "I've got you and Jeannie."

"We're not enough, Dad. I can tell you're not happy." I so want to talk to him about his drinking, but I'm too chicken.

"I'm just fine."

"You're only forty-five. It's been seven years since Mom died. Time to think about moving on." Dad shifts uncomfortably in his seat. "What about online dating?" I surprise myself by blurting this out.

"Online dating?" Dad looks at me like I have four heads.

"How else are you going to meet a woman your age? You rarely go out, even for a beer with your work guys. You putter around the acreage, sort your tools, take Ruby for walks, bird-watch. That's it. You don't even ski or hike anymore."

"You make me sound so pathetic."

"You are far from pathetic, Dad. There are hundreds of women out there who would love to meet a guy like you. You're smart, handsome, a talented carpenter, you have two amazing daughters..."

Dad almost cracks a smile. If it wasn't dark out, I bet I could see him blushing.

"Please, Dad. I'll help you write your profile." I try and give him my best pleading look, but now that my face has been rearranged, I'm not sure if I'm pulling it off.

"I'll think about it." Dad looks out his window.

I clap my hands like an idiot.

***

I've been in bed for over an hour reading my bio textbook, trying to study cell differentiation and development in the human organism for the upcoming exam. My focus is way off. All I can think about are the words *bear* and *bait*. Jarret and Thomas in our hiking group used to joke that whichever one of us girls had our period was the bear bait. I grab my iPhone and hold down the home button to chat with Siri. "Bears attracted to menstruating women," I say into my phone.

"Let me have a look," Siri says. "Okay, I found this on the web for 'bears attracted to menstruating women.'" I scroll through the list of links and read an article on *LiveScience.com*. Apparently neither black bears nor brown bears are attracted to menstruating women, but polar bears are. Weird.

"I am bear bait," I say to Siri.

"Okay, I found this on the web for 'I am bear bait,'" Siri says. There's a website that sells bear lures and scents to hunters. *We are committed to making your bear hunts a success!* There is a list of all the products they sell "for animal consumption only": pie fillings, buttercream icing, peanut butter, and imitation maple syrup. What the…?

I hear a ping, a Messenger notification. Someone with the handle UR SO FN UGLY sends me a meme. Gee, I wonder who it could be. Frankenstein's monster is strapped to a table with these words written underneath: *Don't feel bad, don't feel blue, Frankenstein was fucking ugly too.* It takes my breath away. I close my laptop and push it to the far side of my bed. Hug my knees and rock. I remember the day my bandages came off and all I could think about was how much the zigzag of scars all over my face looked like Adam, the creature in the movie *I, Frankenstein.*

FEVER

I walk out of the girls' change room into the gym. I had to practically beg Ms. Wong, the girls' phys ed teacher, to let me take
this class. She worried about my injuries, especially my leg, but
I would rather be moving my body than sitting at a desk for the next
few months. Dad finally fixed the brakes on Rusty—name says it
all—my 1992 Mazda, so I drove myself to school early to change into
my gym strip without anyone around. I wish I'd worn a turtleneck
under my T-shirt to hide the gruesome scars on my chest. A clear
picture of how the bear's claw swiped me from my shoulder across
my chest. My once muscular legs are as skinny as bamboo shoots.
My shorts don't fully cover the scar on my upper right thigh.

A few guys sitting on the bleachers look over at me and smile. I
wave awkwardly, feeling practically naked in my T-shirt and shorts. I
pretend I'm scratching my head, but I'm really trying to hide my face
with my hand. What are guys doing in the gym when it's the girls'
phys ed? My whole body is freezing, covered in goose bumps with
purple splotches. I feel even more embarrassed that my nipples, like

frozen peas, are sticking out of my flimsy T-shirt. Another reason I should have worn a turtleneck. More guys come in, including Liam, with Serena glued to his side, talking his ear off. He looks mildly interested in the conversation. Then come Grace, Briar, Ms. Wong, and Mr. Harris, the guys' teacher. A whole bunch more people crowd into the gym. Grace and Briar walk toward me.

Grace says, "Did you forget?"

"Forget what?" I ask.

Briar looks me up and down, obviously not impressed with what she sees. "It's social dance today. We're joining classes."

"Shit." I feel like such a fool. I'm the only one in gym strip. I make a dash for the change room door, but Ms. Wong stops me. "The class is starting right now, Abby. No time to change." I turn, head down to avoid any stares or snickers, and stand close to Grace.

"Okay, everyone, your attention here, please. Boys number off starting with one, girls do the same. Then find the person with the same number as you. There may be more boys, so we'll just have to make do."

As the numbering starts, my heart sinks when Mason, red-eyed with a silly grin, bounds into the gym and jumps into line with the other guys. I'm number seventeen. Everyone mills about calling out their number. I pray so hard that Mason isn't number seventeen. He's not. But Liam is. What are the odds? Liam stands near but turns his back to me. I'm now shivering, so cold and totally mortified.

"OK class, today you're going to learn how to foxtrot. As I'm sure most of you know, this is a traditional ballroom dance," Mr. Harris says.

"This is stupid. Why do we have to learn such a lame dance?" Justin asks.

"So you can dance with your mother on your wedding day," Ms. Wong says.

"I'm never getting married," Justin says, crossing his arms.

"Then pretend you're the next contender on *So You Think You Can Dance.*" Lots of laughs, groans, and rolled eyes. "Come on, let's just have some fun with this."

Briar and Mason are partners, Grace and Justin, Serena and a new guy I don't know. Ms. Wong and Mr. Harris demonstrate.

"Traditionally, men lead and women follow in this dance. To demonstrate, I'll be the leader," says Mr. Harris. "But I'm all about equal opportunity, so you decide who leads and who follows. Stand facing your partner, about an arm's length apart, and notice our hand and arm positions." Ms. Wong and Mr. Harris go through the steps very slowly, like drawing invisible boxes with each sequence. Then they speed it up. Harris steps on Wong's toes, which makes everyone laugh.

"Now it's your turn. I'll let you practice for a few minutes before I put on the music. Face your partners," Ms. Wong says.

Liam turns to me but won't look me in the eye. I put my left hand on his shoulder, he puts his right hand on my waist. I'm sure he can feel my back ribs sticking out, which makes me squirm. We hold our other hands.

"Your hand's like ice," he says.

"Sorry, I'm a little underdressed for this class."

"No kidding," he says without a smile.

Great. Now I feel even more self-conscious. Liam and I start the steps. I'm supposed to go forward but go backward, instead, and screw everything up. My bad leg drags a bit. We keep trying and finally get into a stilted rhythm. When everyone's finally getting the hang of it, Mrs. Wong puts on the old 1950s song "Fever" by Peggy Lee. It's slow and sultry.

I look right at Liam's face, his big hazel eyes, the smooth skin on his cheeks, stubble on his chin, but his eyes are focused on the reddish-purple scar on my neck, peeking just above my T-shirt. Gerry and Gus are dance partners and ham it up in an over-the-top, goofy sort of way as they glide gracefully across the gym floor. Mason and Briar dance all crazy-like at super-speed. They bump right into us.

"Well, lookee here. If it isn't the lovebirds," Mason says, making Briar laugh like a ditz.

"Shut up, Mason." Liam glares at him. When Mason found out about Liam and me, I was worried Mason and his crew might go after Liam. Pound the shit out of him. But other than having a vicious verbal spat with Liam, Mason directed most of his hate and rage at me. He's always had a grudging respect for Liam. Maybe it's Liam's confidence, the way he carries himself with such composure and self-assurance. Mature. He's everything that Mason isn't.

For a brief moment, Liam looks right at me, or at least at my good eye. I can tell he feels something, but for the life of me I just can't figure out what that is.

***

I walk to Simon's through the neighbor's property. The western sky is an explosion of pinks and purples as the sun sinks behind the mountains. The Chinook melted most of the snow, and the air smells of damp earth and hay. I hear something or someone behind me on the path, rustling in the bushes. I can't see anything, but a thudding sound is getting closer. My mind first leaps to the grizzly and then to

Mason, when he started stalking me after we broke up. I start to walk faster. Turn around again. I see a large black shadow coming toward me. I run as fast as my legs will go. By the time I get to Simon's, I'm gasping for air. I pound on the door, turn around one more time. Two deer amble out of the bushes by the path.

***

"Do you often have these weird hallucinations?" Simon asks and hands me a heaping bowl of macadamia nut gelato. We sit on the most comfy leather couch on the entire planet. Every time I sink my body into the corner, I give thanks to the cow that gave up its hide to cover this couch.

"I just get spooked sometimes, that's all. Give me a break. Besides, it's getting dark out." I spoon a heaping amount of deliciousness into my mouth and let it sit there.

Simon flips through a menu on the eighty-five-inch TV with five thousand satellite channels. "Where shall we go tonight? Denmark, Latvia, Jordan, or Columbia?"

"Not really feeling like a movie tonight."

Simon puts the remote down. "Okay, what's up?" He scoops a fudgy bit into his mouth.

"I know you think grad is stupid, and you say you don't want to go, but—"

"No way, Abby. As I've told you before, I'm not going. Besides, I thought you and Liam made a blood pact to go to grad together no matter what."

"We did make a promise, and I know Liam will honor it, but…"

"So I'm your backup date in case Liam bails?"

"Of course not. I just want my best friend celebrating grad with me. Maybe we can double-date."

"That would be difficult considering I do not—and will not—ever have a grad date," he says.

"There must be someone you want to ask. What about Rachel in your math class?"

"Rachel? Have you lost your mind?"

"What's wrong with her?"

"Absolutely nothing. That's what's wrong," he says, heaping ice cream onto his spoon. "She's way out of my dating pool. If I actually had a dating pool." He stuffs the spoon into his mouth.

"Don't sell yourself short, Simon. You've got your own kind of hot stuff going on."

Simon rolls his eyes. "The answer is still a definitive no."

"Could be a blast, seeing who hooks up with who. We can make fun of the Sticky Hive behind their backs."

"Why are you so obsessed with going to grad? You don't even want to be seen around the hallways at school, let alone getting selfied to death," says Simon.

"I know, I know. I sound like a ditz. It's just that I've missed out on so much these past months and I've decided I don't want to miss out on grad."

"Jackson and I were thinking of going to Electric Circus."

"A video arcade? On grad night?"

"Why not? Works for us."

"Please come." I give him my best pleading look.

"Not going to happen, Abby."

***

When I get home, the house is dark. Dad's truck is gone. Ruby greets me at the door with her wagging tail and happy whines and won't let me pass until I give her tons of loving. She follows me upstairs to my room. I open up my laptop and click on a file I haven't opened in well over a year. It's filled with posed photos of Serena, Grace, and me, taken in the fall of grade eleven. When Serena's mom was away in Palm Springs, we raided her closet full of designer clothes and pranced around pretending to be models in a photo shoot, taking turns snapping one another's pictures. I blow up a photo of me looking all full of myself, with bright-red pouty lips and a short silky black dress. A weird feeling tugs me in different directions. I long to go back to how I was, how I looked in these pictures, but I also have sharp pangs of shame for being as shallow as I was. Deep down, am I a total fraud? I lie on the bed, close my eyes, and try to chase away all the crappy feelings. I fall fast asleep.

When I wake up, I hear the TV on downstairs. Dad's home watching old family videos. He has a glass in his hand and a half-empty bottle of Scotch on the table in front of him.

"Oh, you're here," Dad says. Ruby curls up on the rug at his feet.

"Yup."

His attention turns back to the family movies. Mom and Dad are in Banff loading backpacks with food and camping supplies.

"How old was she in this video?"

Dad presses pause. "It was when we first met, so probably around twenty-three, twenty-four." I can almost smell the alcohol seeping through his pores. When he reaches for the bottle to fill up his glass, I'm disappointed in him.

On the TV screen my mom is frozen in time. "She was so beautiful," I say.

"That she was." He stares at her image and un-pauses the video. "This was when we hiked the Jasper Skyline. I'll never forget waking up to a foot of snow—and it was the August long weekend. Your mom, of course, had read the weather report and warned me about snow, but I talked her into going anyway. The whole hike down the mountain, all I heard was, 'I told you it was going to snow, but you wouldn't listen to me.'"

"She did love being right, didn't she?" I say.

"Can you imagine her armed with Internet on a cell phone?"

"She would've been the Google queen, looking up every disputed fact." We both laugh. The video changes to Dad holding Jeannie as a baby. "Aw, look at her," I say. "Chubby baby."

"What about you?" Dad fast-forwards the video to me as a baby, big round cheeks, in my mother's arms. "She sure loved being a mom."

"I still miss her so much," I say.

Dad nods, takes a big gulp of Scotch, and keeps watching the images of mostly Jeannie and me growing up. There's a video of me in elementary school, playing Scarecrow in *The Wizard of Oz*, hamming it up. The next video is me in middle school playing the lead in *Annie*. My reddish hair in tight curls, my rosy-red cheeks, dancing and singing at the top of my lungs. No inhibitions about being in front of an audience. There are a few more short unmemorable shots of me onstage in grades nine and ten. Then the video switches to my performance as Joan of Arc. A monologue. I'm alarmed and angry in this scene. I acted it well. My voice was just right.

I stop hearing the sound and can only see myself on the TV. The old me. My body is whole. My face is expressive, without bumpy red scars. I have a left cheek. My right eye opens just fine. My smile is normal, not crooked. I was so happy back then, living the life of an ordinary, pretty, teenager.

"You are a born actor, that's for sure," Dad says, breaking the spell.

"*Was*, Dad. Those days are long gone."

"You're almost finished high school. You need to start thinking about your future."

"What future?" I meant this to be my inside voice.

Dad turns to me. "You know there's money put away for both you and Jeannie to go to university."

"Maybe you should use the money you saved for my education to pay bills. I see how stressed out you are all the time."

"You've got to move forward with your life, Abby."

"What about you, Dad? All you do is work and drink. That's about it. And there's been more drinking than working lately. You are always miserable. And so distant. Sometimes I feel like you look right through me."

Dad aims the remote at the TV like a gun and fires it off. He stands up. I've hurt him and I feel terrible.

"Dad, I'm sorry. I shouldn't have—" He waves me off and walks away.

I head up to my room feeling too crappy for grizzly research but I wake up my computer anyway. A Messenger notification pings. Another meme from UR SO FN UGLY. The picture matches the message: *You're so fucking ugly, you have to put a bag on your head to get your dog to hump your leg!* My eyes slowly flood with tears that spill out down my cheeks. After we broke up, Mason sent me nasty texts and Facebook messages, but they stopped after I ended up in the hospital. Obviously he's revived his vendetta against me. I take another look at the meme and all I see is myself in that picture, with a bag over my head. I try to delete the message, but I'm too wound up to figure out how. My body heaves as I sob into my pillow.

When no more tears come, I wipe my wet face and blow my nose. I walk down the hall to Dad's room. There's still a light on, so I knock on the door.

"Dad?" I knock again.

He opens the door a crack. Looks like hell.

I say, "I'm sorry for what I said."

"Things haven't been easy for either of us. Let's both try to move forward as best we can." Dad opens the door wide enough to stick his arm out and put his hand on my shoulder. It feels warm and gentle. I can't remember the last time he touched me. I put my hand on his.

TORMENTED

From across the drama room, Mason shoots me a look so vile it gives me the shivers. Why won't he just leave me alone?

"Since Carter and Leon are the only one-act play team to have submitted both their first and second drafts early, they will begin their rehearsal today." Mr. Owen tents his fingers and paces back and forth at the front of the class. "As for the rest of you," he looks around the class, rests his eyes on me, "I need a draft emailed to me by tomorrow." He turns to Carter and Leon. "Before you start rehearsal, give us a little background about why you chose to write this particular play."

Owen walks to the back of the class. Leon and Carter go to the front of the room.

"Our play is called *Imagine That*," says Leon. His black hair rests on his shoulders. "The story is loosely based on our childhood experiences. Strangely enough, we both had imaginary friends." Everyone laughs.

"My family moved from Melbourne, Australia, to Calgary when I was ten," Carter says, still with a trace of an Aussie accent. "I was such a short, scrawny little guy and I looked about half my age. Everyone picked on me. Even the girls. I became the class clown to win over friends. And when that didn't work, I always had Herman, my imaginary friend."

Leon takes over. "Growing up on a farm, my siblings and cousins were all into 4-H Club, horseback riding, skiing in the winter, and swimming in ice-cold lakes in the summer. From day one I was so different from pretty much everyone, a total sports klutz, and all I wanted to do was read. I started reading when I was four years old, always had my nose in a book. I got seriously picked on by my siblings and friends because of it. My imaginary friend, Theodore, understood me and loved reading, too."

The rehearsal begins. Leon sits on a chair intently reading *War and Peace*, while Carter darts around, stuffing notebooks and dog-eared papers into his backpack.

"Merlin," Carter says with his hand out, "give me my book."

"Go away," says Leon, a.k.a. Merlin, who doesn't take his eyes off the page.

"My book. Now!"

"I'm just at the Battle of Borodino—the big showdown between the Russian and French troops."

"Give it to me." Carter grabs at the book, but Leon gets up and darts around to avoid him. Some hilarious physical humor. "Geez, Merlin!"

"What are you going to do? Tell Mommy?" Leon says.

"Yeah, right. Like I'll say, 'Hey Mom, remember my imaginary friend, Merlin? Well, he's being an annoying nitwit—as usual.'" Carter tries to retrieve the book again, but Leon keeps deking Carter out when he tries to grab it. They play it up. Laughs from the class.

Dax and Mason wear silly grins and laugh too loud. No big secret they were smoking up before class. I wish *they* were imaginary.

"Your mom knows who I am. I mean, you invented me when you were three years old," Leon says. "I think she might actually believe I exist."

"You do exist. But only in my twisted brain. I was supposed to stop believing in you years ago." Carter swipes at the book Leon holds up high. "Just give me my book or I'm going to be late for school because of you. Again!"

Leon suddenly looks serious. He closes the book and stares blankly into space, holding his chin with his hand. Carter angrily grabs the book and stuffs it in his backpack. He sits down to put on his runners.

"So, if you stop believing in me, does that mean I'll no longer exist?" Leon asks.

"That would be my guess."

Leon looks worried. He quickly squats down and helps Carter tie his shoelace, sucking up big time. "Remember when we started that werewolf farm and you sold imaginary werewolves to your grade four class?"

Carter laughs—so do the rest of us. "Yeah, I made about a buck-fifty that day," he says.

We all clap when their rehearsal is over—it was well written and acted. Funny premise—an imaginary friend having an existential crisis.

"Okay, now for the pièce de résistance." Owen looks around the class, raises his eyebrows up and down. "Theater on the Edge has offered to stage the best play from our graduating class in its summer festival." I let out a gasp. Lots of *woo-hoos* and excited expressions. Theater on the Edge performs poetry, modern dance, fringe, music, satire, and just plain weird, thought-provoking stuff. I've always dreamed of acting with the troupe.

"It behooves you, my dear students, to be imaginative, to color outside the lines, to be edgy," he says. "Whoever's performance is chosen will also be offered a summer internship with this very prestigious Calgary theater company. Don't screw up this incredible opportunity."

I look around the class. Everyone is excited. There are a lot of talented people in this class. I want a chance at the internship, but can I pull it off? Would they even consider accepting someone with a disfigured face? If Theater on the Edge did choose me, would I have to put off my surgery this summer?

After class, Dax follows me out of the drama room and we both start down the stairs. On the first landing, Mason and his stoner posse are teasing Leon, blocking him from going down the stairs. Leon is easily six inches shorter than all of them.

Mason sees me. "Well, look who's here." I try to head back up the stairs, but Dax stands in my way, towering over me.

"I think you should ask Bear Bait to grad, Leon," Mason says. This makes the stoners laugh even louder.

Leon glances at me, looking mortified, and I don't blame him. Me as a grad date—could there be a greater insult?

"Don't listen to these losers," I say to Leon.

"Come on, Leon. I can almost guarantee Bear Bait doesn't have a date yet. What do you say?" All the guys are still laughing.

"Fuck off," says Leon as he tries to push his way past. But Mason and Dax grab Leon under each arm and pretty much carry him in front of me.

"Ask her, Leon," Mason says.

"Leave him alone," I say with as loud a voice as I can.

"Shut the fuck up, Bear Bait," Mason says.

"You're still mad at me—I get it."

"Yeah, I am. For slutting around on me." Mason puffs out his chest like a tough guy.

"Leon's done nothing to you. Just let him go." I surprise myself by how strong I sound.

Leon looks terrified. I try to give him an apologetic look. Teachers' voices can be heard on the landing below us. Finally, Mason gestures to Dax and they let go of Leon. He doesn't look at me as he runs down the stairs.

My body is trembling. Mason looks me up and down. "At least there's one good thing about your body. It isn't as ugly as your face." Again, Dax and the other guys crack up.

Mason lets me by, but then Dax grabs my arm.

I say, "Dax, what's going on? We used to be friends."

"Friends? You kidding me? Last year you would barely give me the time of day. Looked down your snobby nose at me like I was a piece of garbage. Thought you were hot shit, didn't you? Well, now look at you." I try to shake out of his grip, but he holds my arm even harder.

I finally shake him off and watch as he stands beside Mason. Dax copies Mason's gesture of rolling his shoulders back and sticking his chest out in a tough-guy kind of way. I can't help but compare Dax to Briar, mimicking the King and Queen Bees. I race down the stairs. I run down the hall right past Schultzy's office, right past the principal's office, and right past the gym, where I hear 1950s Elvis music. No way am I in any shape for social dance. With my luck I'd get Mason as a partner. I push open the front door of the school and head for my car.

***

Curled up in the fetal position, I lie on my bed listening to "For Emma" by Bon Iver while Ruby sleeps beside me, snoring softly. Such great melancholy music, but the tears just won't come. A shame because I feel desperate for a release right now. I grab my phone. "Siri, what should I do about being bullied?"

"Here's what I found on the web for 'What should I do about being bullied.'"

There are scads of websites, but I read through one that says: *Standing up for yourself isn't about fighting back with force. Instead, it means doing your best not to give the bully the attention they're looking for. Stay calm. Tell them to stop or else just ignore them. If you can, walk away. Try talking to a parent, a teacher, the school principal, or the guidance counselor. If bullying happens on the Internet, don't respond to the message. Try blocking the social networking page.*

I flop back on my bed. Talking to someone about bullying sounds like advice for little kids, not someone who is ready to graduate from high school. Someone who's almost an adult. With my new face, I'll have to deal with jerks the rest of my life. Am I going to continue to be a victim or is it time to stand up for myself? I wonder if I can talk to Mason in a reasonable way to stop this shit. If only I were close to someone they looked up to. I sit up and grab my phone again.

"Siri, does Liam still love me?"

"Interesting question."

"Will I ever find love, Siri?"

"Maybe you're looking for love in all the wrong places." Way to go, Siri.

My life is reduced to conversing with my cell phone. I drop my phone in my purse and open up a new Word doc on my laptop. I start writing.

Tormented
by Abby Hughes

It all started with a hiking trip. Little did I know when I woke up that morning my life would change forever. As the days and months have worn on, it turns out the grizzly bear was the least of my worries. Human beings have now become my most deadly predators, which means I'm done for.

I write for over an hour. All my thoughts and feelings come pouring out of me in a monologue about what it's like to be ugly, scared, and bullied. The set will be simple. A chair. Maybe a few different hats or masks, depending on which part of me is talking. Who knows? I read it over and am pleased with my first draft. I email it to Mr. Owen.

A text bloops. I rummage through my purse for my phone. I find the brochure from the doctor's office. *Facing It: Supporting people with facial differences.* It's Thursday, which means there's a meeting tonight in Calgary. The text is from Grace.

Missed u at phys ed. U ok?

Headache

Poor u

I'll live

Market mall tomorrow after school-mom letting me borrow her Volvo

Just us?

Serena and Briar too

How can I face the Sticky Hive after hearing them trash me in the washroom? It still stings. A lot.

I don't think so

Come on Abbs, it will be like old times

It will never be like old times, but I feel so lonely. So desperate for some kind of normal, and I miss Grace like crazy.

No, but thanks

No is not an option-you're coming

I hesitate for a long while.

K

Cu 2morrow

FACING IT

I enter a large meeting room in Calgary's downtown library. A few people are milling about, and others are seated facing a podium at the front. A woman in her early thirties comes toward me, smiling. She has a birthmark that looks like dark red wine stained most of her face and part of her neck. Even so, she's quite pretty.

"I'm Nadine," she says.

"Hi, I'm Abby."

"Is this your first Facing It meeting?"

"Yeah."

"Well, welcome. Great night to come. We have a guest speaker, so I hope you enjoy it. If you'd like to hear about upcoming events, write your email address on our list on the back table. There is coffee, tea, and cookies there, too, if you'd like." Nadine goes off to greet others.

I head for the snack table and write down my name and contact info. I take a cookie off the plate, turn, and scan the room. Some faces are more deformed than mine, others less so. I see the same healing surgical scars on other people that I have on my face. I catch myself gawking, judging—exactly what I hate other people doing to me—but I can't help myself. One guy looks like his face was made of wax, which melted into a permanently droopy position, his chin almost touching his chest. He struggles to keep a cookie in his gaping mouth. I also spot a boy about twelve who has growths that look like big clumps of purple clay glued to one whole side of his face, covering right over his eye. A girl about my age catches me staring at the boy and I'm embarrassed. "My guess is neurofibromatosis," she says as she pours a coffee. "New to the freak show?" From the side, her face looks normal.

"Ah, I guess," I say. She turns around and I see that the other side of her face and neck have been badly burned—her skin looks like crinkled pink and red tissue paper.

"I'm Jade."

"Abby."

Jade checks out the scars on my cheek and forehead. "Nice work. Dr. Baker?"

"Van der Meer."

"I hear she's pretty good, too."

I nod and take another bite of my cookie.

"So, what's your story?" Jade asks and takes a sip of coffee. This conversation feels weird but strangely appropriate. Sharing war stories.

"A bear."

"Yeah, right."

"True story."

Jade's face lights up. "You were mauled by a bear?"

"Yup, a grizzly." I say this a little too proudly.

"Shit. A grizz?" Jade looks impressed. "Most people don't live to tell that story."

"You'd be surprised." I won't tell her how many dozens of YouTube videos I've seen and tons of articles I've read on survivors of bear attacks.

"The next asshole who asks me what happened to my face, I'm so gonna tell them I wrestled with a grizzly bear."

"What did happen?" I gesture to Jade's face, since we're already showing and telling.

"Car accident. Drunk driver."

"Geez, I'm sorry."

"I was the drunk driver," Jade says very matter-of-factly.

I'm tempted to ask for details, but Nadine is at the podium. "Everyone, please take your seats." Jade and I sit together near the back of the room.

"I'm glad to see such a great turnout tonight for our special speaker, who came all the way from Toronto," Nadine says. "She is an advocate, a counselor, a motivational speaker, and one of the co-founders of Facing It. We're very happy to have her with us here in Calgary tonight. Please welcome Heather McLaughlin." Everyone claps.

"Holy shit," Jade says quietly when she sees Heather. I'm both shocked and strangely fascinated as Heather approaches the podium.

"Cherubism," Jade whispers in my ear.

"What's that?"

"Weird genetic disorder. Someone who used to come to this group had it." I wonder if Jade is as obsessed with researching facial deformities as I am with researching grizzly bears.

Heather's face looks way too big for her head, like she's wearing a larger-than-life cartoon mask—with bulgy eyes and an enormously large square chin. Something you'd see in an animated movie. Here I go again, gaping. Judging.

"Hello and thank you for inviting me to speak to you this evening." Heather clicks on the projector and an image of a beautiful, flawless young woman appears. "We live in a society that is obsessed with outward beauty," Heather says. "We are continually bombarded by unrealistic images of beauty on TV, billboards, social media, and in films and magazines." The large screen behind her shows images of stick-thin runway models, movie and TV stars. "Images of celebrities set an impossible standard, especially for people like some of us here who have facial differences."

Heather uses the word *difference* rather than *disfigurement*. Or *deformity*—the word I usually use to describe myself. Heather walks to one side of the small stage and talks to that side of the audience.

Another photo comes on the screen. A grid, like graph paper, superimposed on a woman's face. "One anthropologist discovered that an incongruity of a little over one-thousandth of an inch in the placement of a facial feature triggers something in the brain that makes us do a double take. As a rule, we humans do not like asymmetry."

I had never thought about beauty or attractiveness in a scientific way before.

So what does all this mean for us asymmetrical types?" Chuckles from the audience. "Well, we get a lot of stares, that's for sure. And some people think that because we look different, we also have a mental deficiency. Anyone experience that?" Lots of nods.

***

"So, it's all about symmetry, eh?" I say as Jade and I walk to the parking lot.

"Yeah, but she failed to mention the studies that show attractive people are considered more likable, have more dates, get fewer convictions in serious crimes, and are more likely to get hired for jobs than less attractive people."

An Asian woman in her late twenties walks toward us. "Have a good look at this girl," Jade says.

Long, silky, black hair, perfect skin, and just the right amount of makeup. We turn around when she passes to see a perfect little bum in her skinny jeans.

"Okay, if you were a landlord renting out an apartment—especially if you were a man—would you rent it to Miss Perfect or Inferno Face?"

I get a sudden gut reaction of my own bias. Shit. "Point taken," I say.

"It will always be an uphill battle for us, I'm afraid," Jade says.

I take in this new information. "Do you come to these meetings regularly?" I ask.

She shrugs. "Every now and then. I'm not really a group therapy kind of girl. Like, yeah, our faces are fucked up, but at some point you just have to put on your pointy big-girl boots and kick life's ass."

"I'm not there yet."

"How long ago, since the bear?" Jade asks.

"Just over nine months."

"Not that long really. Totally sucks to be pretty one day and not so pretty the next, eh?" Jade unlocks her car and opens the door. "Good luck with everything. Maybe I'll see you again." She gets in and starts her car.

I walk to my car. A slideshow plays in my mind of all the different faces I saw tonight.

AA CUP

The bio class lights are dimmed and a video plays on the screen. A cartoony male and female face each other. "Human reproduction involves sexual intercourse between a man and a woman," the female's voice on the video says. This gets hoots and laughs from the class, and a stern look from Jessop. Serena whispers something in Liam's ear and they both chuckle.

Mr. Jessop pauses the video. "Are you in grade five, or what? Grow up."

"Is this a grade five video, or what?" Paul says. Lots of nodding heads. When everyone settles down, Jessop restarts the video.

"In this diagram, you will see the male reproductive organs." A computer drawing of a naked male, waist down, side view, penis dangling, with all the parts named: vas deferens, urethra, ejaculatory duct…

As the video plays, I look over at Liam, remembering the first time he and I stood naked in front of each other, alone at his grandpa's cabin in Bragg Creek, where he practically lives on weekends, and sometimes even during the week.

"The male reproductive organs operate together to produce sperm and other substances that are found in semen…" says the video girl.

Liam and I just stood there for about five minutes and observed each other's bodies, not in a sexy way. At least not at first. I took a close look at his penis. I'd never seen a real, live penis before. It just hung there all soft and shriveled. I remember thinking the skin on the end looked like Darth Vader's helmet, but I didn't tell Liam that. Remembering this, I cover my mouth with my hand to stifle a laugh, but instead I make a sound like I'm spitting water out of my mouth. People turn and stare at me.

"Tissues in the penis fill with blood and the penis becomes rigid during sexual arousal…"

In my warped brain, all I can see on the screen is Darth Vader's helmet on one side and an arrow pointing to the tip of a penis on the other. Can't help myself—I'm laughing so hard I'm gasping for breath. Now everyone turns around and looks at me, including Liam, which makes me laugh even louder. Others start to laugh, too.

Jessop pauses the video again. "Abby." He's so not impressed with me. I pick up my books and purse and hurry out of the classroom, still laughing my ass off.

***

"Mason has always creeped me out—even before you went out with him," Grace says as we drive down the township road toward Calgary. "I could never really get what the attraction was."

"No one ever poured on that much attention and affection and compliments. I got totally sucked up in it. And the gifts—flowers, chocolates, dinners, movies, jewelry. I felt like some kind of goddess around him. That is, until it turned weird."

"Weird? It was Stephen King bizarre! He went mental whenever you 'liked' any other guy's posts on Facebook. He hated it whenever you went to the mountains. You missed more than a few backpack trips because he couldn't handle that you'd be with other guys for the whole weekend. Hell, he was even jealous of the time you spent with me and your other girlfriends."

"Okay, you're right. It was messed up."

We arrive in the city limits. I look out the window at the cookie-cutter houses, one after another after another.

"Shit, Abby. He's not right in the head. I'm pretty sure he meets every trait of a sociopath—he probably even tortures small animals for kicks. I really think you need to tell someone what's going on."

"I know Mason. It would just make things even worse."

"But this could easily go beyond bullying, Abbs. I'm worried for you."

My self-loathing is alive and well. There's not much Mason has said to me that I haven't already said to myself. "We only have a few more months of school left and then hopefully I will never have to see him again."

"He's obsessed with getting back at you. What if he never lets up?"

"Then I guess I'll deal with it then. Promise me you won't say anything to anyone."

Grace looks over at me. I know this is a promise she doesn't want to keep, but she nods.

***

Grace and I meet Serena and Briar at Victoria's Secret. As we approach them, they look at each other with wide eyes. It's so obvious they don't want the freak tagging along.

"You didn't tell us Abby was coming," Serena says to Grace, giving her a WTF look. Briar mimics Serena's look.

"I didn't think I had to tell you that I asked *our* friend to come along," Grace says. Suddenly my skin feels all itchy and two sizes too small. I just want to bolt.

"Well, we're all here now," Serena says as unenthusiastically as humanly possible. She turns and walks into the lingerie store with Briar close at her heels.

Grace sighs, gives me an apologetic look, and follows. The three of them immediately start slapping the racks. I wander around not knowing where to start; I haven't bought underwear in way over a year. Besides, in this store, I could totally blow my now meager clothing allowance that's supposed to last for months. When times were better, I used to be so into all of this, used to love shopping with Serena and Grace. I pick up a red, lacy G-string thongy thing (Simon calls it butt floss). The triangle of fabric is so tiny I can't imagine it covering, well, anything. Then there's the Cheeky Panty. Cheeky indeed! A saleslady comes up to me.

"Everything on the tables is half off." She speaks loudly and slowly, as if I'm deaf and a dimwit too. "And the new items are on the far wall." Now she's right in my face, smiling weirdly. "Let me know if I can help you with anything." In her Facing It talk, Heather mentioned sometimes being treated as though she has an intellectual disability because of her facial difference, but it's never happened to me before now. Probably because I've pretty much sequestered myself at home for months.

"No, thanks, I'll be fine just looking around on my own." The woman nods and looks surprised I can articulate a full sentence.

Soon Grace, Serena, and Briar have armfuls of bras. "Grab a few to try on, Abbs," Grace says and follows the others to the change room. I feel so out of place. I've become a bone rack over the past nine months. My breasts have shrunk into withered little prunes—I barely need a bra anymore. But to be a sport, I pull a few random AA-cup bras off the discount table.

In the change area, Briar is already in front of the communal mirror wearing only panties and a heavily padded push-up on top. Her arms are dotted with freckles. She squishes her breasts together to make even more cleavage and looks at herself from all sides. Serena and Grace come out of their change rooms to check out their bras, which look identical to Briar's. Grace's white, lacy bra stands out against her deep-brown skin and jet-black hair. A stark contrast to Serena's pale skin and white-blond hair. I look at all three of them. Perfectly symmetrical faces and flawless bodies. I notice the three have matching belly-button rings with a turquoise stone.

Briar takes a long look at herself in the mirror. She turns around but still looks in the mirror. "My ass is getting so flabby."

"It is not," says Grace.

"Just look at it."

"Your ass looks just fine, Briar," Grace says.

Serena checks out her bra. "My mom told me she'd pay for a boob job as my grad present."

"What?" I say. "You've got to be kidding me."

"She thinks my breasts are already starting to sag." Serena holds them up with both hands. "Said that I should deal with the problem while I'm young, before I go to university, because it's only going to get worse—especially if I ever have kids. She said breastfeeding is the worst possible thing you can do to your breasts."

"That's such bullshit," Grace says. "Your mom is projecting her own anxiety about aging, that's all."

"Sounds like someone's been watching daytime talk shows," Briar says to Grace. "If my mother offered me a boob job I would jump at the chance." Briar's still checking herself out in the mirror.

Serena looks at her beautiful self in the mirror. She looks down at her boobs, frowns, and sighs. Grace shakes her head. She and I share a look.

"Your turn to try one on," Grace says to me.

I go into the change room, whip off my T-shirt and sports bra, and put on a pink, lacy number. It looks ridiculous on me. My ribs ripple along my chest and stick out underneath the bra. "Abby, come out, let's see it," says Grace from outside my door.

I self-consciously open the door to the change room. Briar takes one look at the scars on my chest.

"Holy fuck!"

"Geez, Briar!" Grace says.

I don't blame Briar—the dark-red scars don't really match with light-pink lace. I quickly shut the door of my change room. Run a finger along the thick, ropy lines on my chest. Sink to the floor.

I hear Briar talking softly, but not softly enough for me not to hear. "God, those scars. And she's so skinny."

"Would you just shut up!" I hear Grace say in a loud whisper.

"Wish I was that skinny," Serena says, not quiet at all.

"Stop trashing yourself, Serena," Grace says.

I try on a few more bras but give up. Nothing is going to help me look even the least bit sexy.

***

We walk through the mall. Serena and Briar walk four giant steps in front of us. They stop at a juice bar and we wait in line. Grace nudges Briar. "Sorry, Abby," Briar says sheepishly. "I didn't mean to…it's just…"

"No worries," I say. "It was an honest response." But my heart still stings like someone poked it with a thousand needles.

We get our smoothies and sit at a table.

"It's crazy that we'll be done high school in a few short months," Grace says.

"What are you three going to do in the fall?" I ask.

"Gap year," says Grace. "I have no idea what I want to do, so I'd rather not rack up student-loan debt."

"Mount Royal University," says Briar. "Nursing, if I can get in."

"UCLA, if my dad will pay for it," Serena says. "Beaches, Hollywood, and hot guys. Oh yeah!"

"What about you, Abbs?" Grace asks.

"Foothills," I say.

"Foothills what?" says Briar.

"Hospital. Foothills Hospital," I say. "More surgery on my face."

"Oh, right," Grace says. The three look at one another and all sip their smoothies at exactly the same time. It's clear I make them uncomfortable.

"Should we go to Blush and look for grad dresses?" Serena says, quickly changing the subject.

"First tell me what I'm going to say to Brandon," Briar says like a drama queen as she plays with her brown ponytail. "He asked me to grad," she says looking right at me, because, of course, Serena and

Grace probably found out a nanosecond after she was asked. "But I really want to go to grad with Keegan."

"Ask Keegan if he'll go to grad with you. If he's already going with someone else, say yes to Brandon," Serena says. Her cheeks indent as she sucks on her straw.

"I forgot to tell you, Grace." Briar grabs her arm. "Mason told me that Dax wants to ask you."

Grace rolls her eyes. "Gawd. I'd rather go on my own."

"On your own? As if…," Briar says, looking at Grace as if she's lost her mind.

"How about you, Abby? Going to grad?" Serena asks.

"Yup." Serena's the last person I would tell about Liam and me. I can't help myself. "What about you?" I ask Serena. "Who are you going to grad with?"

The three of them share a look.

"No one's asked me, so I'm not sure yet," she says. They share another look, and I know who the elephant in the room is. Everyone is quiet, but there's something in the air that could be cut with a knife.

In Blush, I sit on a velvety green chair while the three of them model grad dresses. All I can think about is being home, safe in my room with the covers pulled firmly over my head. I text with Simon.

This is brutally painful

Told u, u r a masochist

Thanks for the reminder

Tear yourself away from the sticky hive and save your soul before it's too late

U r such a drama king

Grace, wearing a beautiful sapphire-blue dress, brings out something to show me.

"Abby, this would look amazing on you. See the neckline?" Thoughtful Grace. The neckline's high enough to cover my scars. In a previous life, I might have been able to pull it off.

"Just not into it today."

Grace sits down on the matching green chair. "I know last year you and Liam talked about going to grad together. Has he said anything to you?"

"Not yet, but he will."

"What if he doesn't? What if he forgot, or if—"

"We vowed to go together, Grace, even if we were broken up. If there's one thing I know about Liam, he's a man of his word. Even if he doesn't want to go with me, I know he will."

"I doubt anyone's going to ask me to grad," Grace says. Dear, sweet Grace. At this very moment some hunky rugby guy is nervously rehearsing an asking-Grace-to-grad script.

As we walk through the mall, a group of four guys about our age walks toward us. Everyone slows down. The guys first check out Serena. She smiles at them coyly and flips her long blond hair back. Then Briar flips her ponytail. Big smiles on the guys' faces. When they see me, they look a bit shocked, nudge one another. One guy makes barfing sounds.

"Beauties and the beast," one of the guys says and the others crack up.

"Assholes," Serena says as we walk past them, but I see her and Briar trying to hide their flirty smiles.

"Don't listen to them," Grace says, linking her arm in mine. In front of us, Briar whispers something to Serena and they both laugh. "Any of them."

In my mind, I keep repeating "it's all about symmetry, it's all about symmetry," but tears well up in my eyes and everything looks blurry.

TALISMAN

It's the highest mountain on Earth, but what's the height of Everest?" Dad says to Jeannie, as we drive along the Trans-Canada Highway toward Banff to have Easter with my grandma, my mom's mom. She's usually away traveling the world—hiking, sailing, volunteering—but she's finally home for a month or two to regroup before she heads off on her next extended trip: Bali. She flew home from Argentina to be with me while I was in the hospital. But as soon as I was released, she was on the next plane out. I need her around and wish she would just stay home.

"You're asking me?" Jeannie says. "This is your weird little game with Abby."

Dad and Jeannie are in the front seat of the truck, I'm in the back. Ruby is curled up on the seat beside me sleeping, her head on my lap. Out my window, the rolling foothills zip by.

"Twenty-nine thousand and twenty-nine feet," I say.

"How can I compete? You two are such geography nerds," Jeannie says.

"Your turn, Abby," Dad says.

"Easy one for Jeannie. What's the highest mountain in Canada?" We're getting close to the mountains and it's making me dizzy. I rest my forehead on the cool window and close my eyes.

"Even I know this one," Jeannie says, "Mount Logan."

"Wow, soon you'll be joining the geography nerd club," Dad says.

"Doubt it. But if you want to talk carbohydrate metabolism and glucose homeostasis, I'm your girl."

"How are your courses going?" Dad asks her.

"So bloody hard. I feel like such a loser in the science faculty, competing with students like Baljinder, who is absolutely brilliant."

"Still aiming for med school?" Dad asks.

"If I can keep my head above water."

The closer we get to the mountains, the more claustrophobic I feel. Like the mountains are going to fall on me. My head's still resting on the window and my eyes are still closed. I ask, "Is Caleb as smart as Baljinder?"

"He's pretty darn smart, too," Jeannie says.

"Who's Caleb?" Dad asks.

***

Jeannie, Dad, and I sit around my laptop at Grandma's kitchen table, scrolling through photos of Dad.

"This is a great picture of you, Dad," Jeannie says. "Makes you look outdoorsy, but not like some weird hermit mountain man." The photo was taken near the Fairmont Banff Springs hotel, with Rundle Mountain towering in the background.

"I like this one better," I say of a photo of Dad sitting on our patio in Springbank. "Gramz, what do you think?"

My grandma puts on her thick reading glasses and looks at the computer over our shoulders.

"He looks like a garden gnome," she says.

"Thanks a helluva lot, Audrey," Dad says, chuckling. Dad seems lighter, more content than I've seen him in months. Maybe it's because we're all together for a change. Or maybe he's finally excited about online dating.

"She asked my opinion," Gramz says and goes back to chopping vegetables for a salad. Ruby waits close by for some food to drop.

"Gramz, even you must think it's time for Dad to date again. It's not as if Mom will ever be erased from our lives or anything," I say.

My grandma smiles at Dad. "I've been telling your father for a few years now that it's time for him to move on with his life. Ellen would want you to be happy, Derek. You deserve it."

Dad nods, smiles back. He goes to the stove and turns down a pot of boiling water.

"We've got to do something different for your profile, Dad," Jeannie says. "All these on Match.com and OkCupid are so boring. I did some research on how to make your profile stand out. Instead of all the blah blah blah, how about using the alphabet with each letter describing something about you?" Jeannie says.

"I like it," I say.

"I'm at your matchmaking mercy on this one," Dad says, poking at the boiling potatoes.

"Okay, A is for…," Jeannie says.

"Artistic. You're pretty artsy, Dad," I say. Jeannie types it into the computer.

"B…bibliophile. You're a reader, right?" Jeannie says and types.

"C is for carpenter," Gramz says. "Women love men who know their way around a toolbox."

"D…dashing," I say.

"Now you're making me blush," Dad says.

"E is for…environmentally conscious," Jeannie says.

"Dinner's almost ready." Dad takes the pot off the stove. "You girls can plan my love life later." He drains the potatoes, adds some butter and milk and starts mashing.

After a big turkey dinner, Dad and Gramz go for a walk along the Bow River while Jeannie and I clean up the dishes. Even knowing that bears are likely just coming out of hibernation and are probably nowhere near town, I can't bring myself to go outside except to run to and from the truck. Being here, right in the mountains, is scaring the crap out of me.

"I know why you don't want to tell Dad. He'd totally freak out, pound down the school door. But you should at least tell Schultzy or Hardy," Jeannie says as she dries the salad bowl.

"They haven't even figured out who wrote *Bear Bait* on my locker, so I doubt they'd be able to find out who's messaging me." I squirt some dish soap into a pot and fill it with hot water.

"Could it be Mason? He wouldn't still be after you, would he?" Jeannie asks.

I shrug.

"I'll never forget when he tried to get into your phone to see who you were texting and went ballistic when he found out you put a passcode on it." Jeannie picks up another bowl to dry. "He sent you all those repulsive texts. And don't get me started about the stalking."

If I told her the extent of Mason's bullying, she would definitely tell Dad. I don't want to risk escalating things even more. After Mason and I broke up, Jeannie caught him in his truck parked at the end of our driveway, looking through binoculars at our house. Told him she'd call the cops if she ever saw him near our house again. *She* never saw him there again, but I did.

"The cops could somehow track down whoever is doing it," Jeannie says.

"I'm definitely not getting the cops involved. I just want to get through the next few months and leave high school behind."

***

I wake up in the middle of the night, my body shaking from a nightmare. Jeannie sleeps soundly beside me. In my dream, I was in my grandma's backyard. The bear was circling me. Growling, baring her teeth. I ran into the woods, leaves crunching, twigs snapping. I tripped, fell hard to the ground. When I turned around, she was bounding toward me, and I knew I couldn't escape. I remember being in this same bed with my mom when she and I visited Gramz. When I couldn't fall asleep, Mom would wrap me in a big hug until I did. I lie back down and put my arm around Jeannie's waist and hold her close.

***

Dad and Jeannie left early this morning to hike Sunshine Meadow and to leave tulips, Mom's favorite flower, at the top. Grandma and I sit in her sunroom and drink coffee while Ruby sleeps in a sunbeam on the rug. The bear figurine is on the coffee table in front of us.

"The bear's now your talisman." Gramz has always been a bit "out there" with her solstice parties, energy clearing, and interest in most things new age. "It's a great honor and responsibility to have Bear walking beside you. She'll speak to you if you listen."

"What do you mean, if I listen?"

"You say she comes to you in your dreams—you can draw power from that. Before you go to sleep, ask her what she wants to share with you."

"Not dreams, Gramz—nightmares. I'm always scared out of my mind. I wake up sweating and shaking."

Gramz takes a sip of coffee, brushes a strand of gray hair behind her ear and weighs her words.

"From ancient times right up to the present, people from all over the world have believed that certain individuals are watched over by animal spirits that act as their 'life guides' or talismans. Some people, including me, believe that talismans can bring strength and wisdom. Maybe that mamma bear is showing you that you have more power and courage than you ever imagined."

"I'm pretty sure I will never feel powerful or courageous ever again in my entire life."

Gramz leans in close, takes my hand, and looks me right in the eyes. "It's time to stop hiding, Abby. Stop cowering from life. You're letting what happened to you take your power away." She picks up the bear figurine and hands it to me. "Don't run away from her—learn to dance with her."

I look closely at the bear and imagine her dancing.

TAMMY

Mr. Owen walks around the class handing back drafts of our monologues and plays. I've got excited butterflies in my stomach. Owen hands me mine, gives me a disapproving look. On the title page of "Tormented" it reads:

Abby,
This isn't a monologue, it's a histrionic rant. I know what kind of writing you're capable of and I want to see that in the next draft.
J. Owen.

My heart sinks. I was so sure I nailed it. I thought I had written everything he asked for: an important event that happened to us, what we've learned, what's important to us.

Obviously not.

I pull the bear figurine out of my purse and hold it.

"I was pretty impressed with some of the writing I read. Others," Owen looks right at me, "I know can do a hell of a lot better. Draft two by week's end. I'm expecting great things, so don't disappoint."

I whisper to the bear, "Tell me what I need to write."

Mason turns, looks at the figurine then at me. I want to give him the finger but decide against it. Don't want to fuel the already smoking-hot fire. I slip the bear back into my purse.

"Tammy, you're up for rehearsal," Owen says and moves to the back of the room.

Tammy goes to the front of the class. "My monologue is called, 'Ten Things You Need to Know About Transitioning.' It doesn't really need a setup." Tammy used to be Jeremy. She used to be a he and has been transitioning since we were fifteen. I first met Jeremy in grade three. He was the only boy in my class who would come over and play dress-up with me. And definitely the only boy I knew who had Barbie's Dreamhouse and Pop-Up Camper.

"Number one. If anyone tells you that transitioning, whether from male to female or female to male, is an easy road, they're lying." Tammy has shoulder-length wavy hair with red and blond high-lights. Wears tons of makeup, but it looks natural in a strange kind of way. Even with the bright turquoise eye shadow. "It will turn your world upside down, kick your ass, and make you obsessively question every little thing in your life.

"Number two. If you're transitioning from male to female like I did, brace yourself for the toxic culture of beauty. The beauty industry makes billions of dollars exploiting women's insecurities about their looks with messages and images aiming to tear down our self-esteem. A few months into my transition, I told my aunt I couldn't wait to see a pretty girl look back at me in the mirror. She said, 'You realize that's never going to happen, right? You're going to look at your reflection and feel as unsatisfied as every other woman.'"

This gets a few uncomfortable, knowing laughs. I can't help but think of the Hive, of me. Tammy goes on to tell about her journey, sometimes funny but more often painful. Trying to tear down the old and rebuild this new person she's become.

"Number ten. Be your authentic self. As someone who is transgender, I spent most of my life pretending to be someone I wasn't to please my family, friends, and society in general. It was exhausting, and I made myself miserable because of it. I hit some very low points where I even contemplated suicide. But the most important thing transitioning has taught me is that life is way too short to worry about what other people think of you. Be who you are. Live out loud in quadraphonic sound. You deserve to live an authentic life."

Tammy's words sink deep into my body. I wonder when I will allow my authentic self to finally show up.

***

It's sunny and unseasonably warm, so everyone sits outside at the picnic tables to eat lunch. The soft wind smells of damp earth. The farmer's field by the school has pools of water where the piles of snow melted, and there's now only splotchy snow on the mountain peaks.

I can't eat with Simon. He and Jackson are showing a girl named Olivia from their engineering electronics class around the school. Her mother just got transferred from Colorado to Calgary, from one oil patch to another. I don't see Grace, Serena, or Briar, but I do see Tammy sitting alone at a picnic table.

"Mind if I sit here?" I ask her.

"Not at all," she says. When she tucks her hair behind her ear, a large silver hoop earring glints in the light.

"Your monologue was great, by the way. So much I didn't know about you, what you've gone through." I take my leftover veggie stir-fry out of my bag.

"Yeah, it was a hard thing to write. Had to relive a lot of those experiences."

I can relate about writing on a subject that dredges up difficult and painful memories.

"Sorry I wasn't there for you, Tammy. I guess I've been on my own planet the past couple of years."

"No worries. I've had a pretty strong network around me." She runs her hand across both cheeks. "What do you think? My facial hair is slowly going away. Too slowly for my liking, but I've just got to be patient."

"Yeah, you're looking great all over." I'm especially jealous of her new perky boobs.

"When you don't like the package, change it."

"Wish it were that easy."

"Sorry, Abby, I didn't mean…"

"Forget about it. It's just me still feeling sorry for myself."

"Must be weird being back at school, eh?" she says, studying the scars on my face curiously—not in an obnoxious way like most people do.

"Yup, it sure is."

"I'll never forget the first day of grade ten when I came to school in a pink poodle skirt with high white boots." Tammy takes a salad container out of her bag. "The last day of grade nine I'd worn my rugby jersey and torn jeans."

"You were so awesome, strutting around the halls, flirting with the guys."

"Thanks to drama class, because I was dying inside—felt *so* incredibly self-conscious. Actually, I hated my body then. But I really played it up with Mason, Rocky View's macho man. Thought he was going to shit himself. But man, did I ever pay for that."

"What happened?" I slurp some bean sprouts.

"You know, typical bullying stuff. Name-calling, spreading rumors, stealing my stuff, nasty Snapchat messages."

"Did you ever tell anyone about it?" I ask.

"Yeah, I did. Schultzy. But then the shit really hit the fan when Mason and Dax got hauled into Hardy's office." Tammy forks her spinach salad.

"What happened?"

"After school one day, they crammed me into a locker in the guys' phys ed change room. Took two hours for Harris to find me."

"Holy shit. Why don't I know this?"

"Next time I saw Mason, I just snapped. Punched the shit out of him—think I broke his nose. He hasn't bugged me since."

"I'm having Mason problems of my own. Maybe I should practice my left hook," I joke.

"I'd help you out, but I don't want any blood on my sage-green cashmere sweater and matching skinny jeans." We both have a laugh. "How well do you know Mason?" Tammy asks.

"We went out in the summer of grade ten and into grade eleven."

"Oh yeah, I remember. That was before Liam." Tammy looks at me knowingly. I wish she, along with everyone else, would catch a serious case of amnesia.

"I was such an idiot." I try to shake the memory from my mind.

"It's none of my business, but what happened between you and Mason?" Tammy asks.

"When Mason and I were still going out, Liam and I hooked up on a backpacking trip. And then we got together another time. I waited too long to tell Mason, and he went apeshit when he found out." I fork a hunk of red pepper. "There was a bunch of other stuff, too, that I won't bore you with. Suffice it to say, it was a very unhealthy relationship."

"We all make mistakes, Abby."

"Yeah, well, mine is coming back to haunt me. The main reason I went out with Mason in the first place was because he was taller than me, had bulging biceps and wheels to drive me around. How shallow is that?"

"Pretty shallow." Tammy breaks into a big smile, which makes me feel a little less horrible about myself. "Not that it's an excuse for being such a dick, but Mason probably told you his parents knocked him around when he was a kid. He was in and out of foster homes for a while."

"Yeah, he told me a little about it." I take another bite. "You don't think Mason would do anything dangerous, do you?"

"You know he spent most of junior high school in juvie?"

"Yeah, I did."

"He set fire to his neighbor's garage, threatened a teacher, and stole a computer from school," Tammy said.

"I didn't hear about that." I'm shocked. The stir-fry turns sour in my stomach.

"I'm surprised he's lasted this long in high school without being locked up again." Tammy gives me a questioning look. "What's really going on with you and Mason?"

"You know, same bullying stuff he did to you. Nothing I can't handle." Quick! Deflect! "So what's Dax's excuse?"

Tammy shrugs. "Blind leading the blind?"

We're quiet for a few minutes, both eating our lunches. From what Tammy has said, ratting out Mason to Schultzy or Hardy will definitely make everything worse. I feel so trapped. *Fuck!*

"Who are you going to grad with?" Tammy asks.

"Liam. You going?"

"Yup, with Charley, and I already bought my dress. Imagine this: salmon chiffon, spaghetti straps, and a plunging neckline."

"Sounds *très* sexy. Good for you, Tammy." I wish I had even a microgram of her courage and self-confidence.

Tammy looks me up and down. "I don't mean to be a bitch or anything, but what happened to you?"

I'm surprised at her comment. "It was on the news, Tammy. The whole world knows what happened to me."

"Not talking about the run-in with the bear. Just that you used to dress so stylishly, in a cool boho kind of way. I always admired your taste in clothes. But now…"

I look down at my hiking shorts and faded T-shirt with a coffee stain on the front. Tammy hands me her phone.

"Plug in your coordinates. You need a makeover."

MAN VERSUS GRIZZLY

After school, I talk Simon into coming to the Calgary Zoo with me. We stand outside the bear enclosure. We're alone, no other visitors around. Although there's a pretty high fence between us and the grizzly bear sleeping in the sun, I stand behind Simon, as if he can somehow protect me if the bear smashes through the reinforced wire.

"Why are we here again?" Simon asks.

"So I can face my fear, try to get some inspiration to write this stupid monologue for drama, whatever."

"That guy's not looking too scary."

But the bear smell brings me right back. Images of her huge paw clawing at me. My head in her mouth. My whole body shivers.

"Let's wake him up. Make it worth your while." Simon yells out, "Hey, Mr. Grizzly, wakey, wakey. Time to get up."

Surprisingly, the bear raises its head and looks over at us.

"That's better," says Simon. The bear slowly hauls its huge body to standing position. Stretches like Ruby does after a nap. "Now we're talkin.'"

The grizzly ambles toward us. My knees feel wobbly. I close my eyes and breathe deeply.

"Look at the guy. He's harmless, like a big puppy."

Still hiding behind Simon, I open my eyes just a sliver. He does look harmless. I shut my eyes again and try to imagine myself in the enclosure with the bear, reaching out to touch his thick fur, feeding him berries out of my hand. That is, until—

"Oh my God, oh my God!" Simon yells. My eyes spring open. The grizzly is now right on the other side of the fence. Simon is truly freaked out. The bear opens its huge mouth in a ferocious growl, showing its long, sharp teeth. "Let's get the hell out of here."

We turn around and run down the pathway as fast as our legs will go. Simon's laughing hysterically. Me, I'm just hysterical.

***

Simon drives us through downtown. Horns honk in the end-of-day traffic. Calgary is so vibrant and interesting compared to our sleepy community. Skyscrapers, hundreds of feet tall, tower over the streets, blocking the sun. Cool graffiti of a colorful dragon covers a large brick building. Buskers play guitars or saxophones on street corners.

"Turns out Olivia also took a summer program at the University of Denver in robotics engineering and programming with VEX," Simon says.

"Hmm." I watch a homeless woman wearing a thin, dirty sweater struggle to push her shopping cart through the slushy snow.

"And she learned ROBOTC software. So jealous."

"Hmm." I haven't seen Simon quite this excited talking about a girl.

"Sorry I'm boring you, it's just that…"

"You met someone who speaks your computer language. I get it."

"Yeah, literally. There are guys—and girls—at school who are interested in engineering and robotics, but none of them know as much as Olivia. She's light-years ahead of both Jackson and me. Did I tell you that last year NASA was interested in her team's design for a robotic arm?"

"Yes, you did. About three times." I can't help but smile as we drive just out of town toward the foothills. The sun is sinking over the mountains in the distance.

"I wonder where she'll go to university this fall. I mean, with her marks she could get in anywhere. Maybe she'll get accepted to the University of Waterloo in computer science like me, or maybe engineering. That's it. Probably software engineering. Or maybe robotics," says Simon.

"If she's American, wouldn't she go to a university in the States?" I ask.

"Of course. You're right. She's brilliant, so she'll probably get in to Harvard or MIT. Geez. I'll be so envious if she does."

"Simon, don't leave me. Can't you just stay in Calgary for university?" I say.

He shakes his head. "No can do, Abby."

I feel so alone already.

***

After dinner, Dad sits in front of his laptop, a glass of Scotch close by. His forehead wrinkles in worry lines as he sorts through a pile of bills. I sit across from him at the kitchen table.

"Dad?"

"Yeah?" He types something into the computer.

"Have you checked the online dating site? Maybe someone has contacted you."

Dad shakes his head. "All I can think about is finding more work, kiddo. And paying these bills." He picks up a piece of paper. His mouth is an upside-down U.

"I could find a job to help out."

"You just focus on getting through the school year. Leave the rest to me." He takes a drink and flips over another bill. But I can see a big weight pulling down his shoulders.

"Dad, please just check the dating site."

He looks up at me. Nods.

"Promise me."

He tries his best to smile. "Okay, I promise."

***

Ruby snores on my bed beside me as I watch a YouTube video titled "Beware: Man vs Grizzly." A grizzly mauls a man lying on the ground while an onlooker just stands there filming it. It soon becomes clear that the man on the ground isn't in danger; he's a bear trainer. The bear sticks its muzzle in the man's chest for a pat, just like Ruby does. The man rubs his head on the bear's chest, and it's clear the bear loves it. The grizzly wraps its huge open mouth around the man's arm and then his head, but in a playful way. They wrestle some more, but the trainer is always in control. The man stands, and the bear rises on its rear legs. They move around in a circle, hands holding enormous paws. I recognize the music as Lyle Lovett's song "Bears" that Dad used to listen to, but doesn't anymore out of respect for me.

I watch this video about a hundred times. I feel scared at first. Not sure what to make of it. Wondering if it's all fake, animatronics. But I soon realize this is a real grizzly bear and a real man. I close my eyes and imagine myself playing, wrestling with the grizzly bear at the zoo, sticking my hand in its fur. The mouth wrapped around my arm, but its dagger-like teeth not piercing my flesh. And when it gets too rough, I hold up my hand for him to stop. I am in control. I am the one in the lead.

I open a blank Word doc.

Dancing with the Bear
by Abby Hughes

JAVA JUNCTION

So then Devin pukes all over this expensive carpet from Turkey or India, and Miles and Brandon have to haul him outside so he doesn't do any more damage," Briar says as she pulls off her phys ed T-shirt. "Eddie's parents will totally freak out. Puke leaves stains on everything. They're so rich and all their stuff is worth a frickin' fortune."

We're in the girls' change room, all sweaty after playing soccer outside on the school field. I rub my bad leg, which aches like crazy.

"You didn't miss a thing, Abby." Grace sits on the bench, unties her soccer cleats, and pulls them off. "A stupid, boring party. Basically, it was the rugby team playing a game of 'Who's more macho?'" Grace air quotes this. "Keegan picked a fight with Miles. Called him a pussy all night for not drinking, even though he was driving. Kept pushing Miles around, literally. Keegan's such an asshole."

"He is not. He just had too much to drink, that's all," Briar says all pissy.

"Oh, I forgot. You're going to grad with him." Grace rolls her eyes at me and puts her cleats in her locker.

"Who else was there?" I ask, dying to know if Liam went.

Grace is on to me. "Liam had to work," she smiles, "but Serena, Justin, Shayla, Gus, and Max were there. As I said, so flipping boring. I was home in bed watching Netflix by ten."

"Well, I had a blast," Briar says, pulling on her skinny jeans.

"That's because you were making out with wannabe tough guy most of the night."

"Jealous?" Briar says.

Grace puts her finger in her mouth and makes gagging noises. She then turns to me. "Wanna hang out?"

"Got something on this aft. Maybe tomorrow?" I say and take my clothes to a private change room.

I drive through the booming metropolis of Bragg Creek, Alberta. Population of about six hundred. Unlike in Calgary where there's a café practically on every corner, out in the sticks we have to drive at least fifteen to twenty minutes for a decent Americano or latte. But it's so worth it.

This will be only my second time back to Java Junction since I got out of the hospital. The first time was last fall when Liam wouldn't answer my texts or phone calls, and I tried to track him down at work. I'm sure he locked himself in the bathroom to avoid me, but Penny, Liam's mom, made me a latte on the house. I asked her for a to-go cup and have never gone back to Java Junction since.

Simon's shiny Jeep is already parked in front. Why did I let him talk me into meeting him here? I could very well run into Liam. If I check in with myself, deep down maybe that's why I agreed to come. It will never be exactly like it was between Liam and me, but maybe we can somehow rejig a friendship. The way he's been avoiding me, I'm having serious doubts.

When I open the door, Penny looks up with a big smile on her face.

"Well look who's here." She comes from behind the counter and wraps me in a big hug. "So good to see you, Abby."

"You, too, Penny."

Her short, spiky hair matches the burnt-orange color painted inside the café. Historical black-and-white photographs of Kananaskis Country and the Elbow River Valley hang on the walls: an old log cabin with a swirl of smoke drifting out the chimney, a man smoking a pipe in front of a fieldstone fireplace, the snowy peaks of the Kananaskis Range, an ancient rusted-out tractor. The rustic wooden furniture makes you feel like you could be sitting right beside that homesteader smoking his pipe over a hundred years ago.

"Liam told me you were back at school. How's it been for you?" Penny asks.

"Meh. But I'm managing."

"He's not here yet, but he shouldn't be too long."

Shit, he *is* working today. I sense another collision of awkwardness coming up.

"I'm actually meeting Simon, but thanks. Could you make me one of your super-delicious double-shot mochas with whipped cream, butterscotch sauce, and chocolate sprinkles?"

"You got it. I should name that drink after you." Penny winks at me and then goes behind the counter and starts grinding the coffee beans.

Simon and Olivia, the new girl, are talking animatedly. Coffee mugs are on the table in front of them. Three women, probably from the new subdivision just outside of town, sit on the comfy retro couch, holding babies while their other kids run around.

"Hey," says Simon as I walk to the table. "Olivia, Abby. Abby, Olivia."

"Hi," I say. "Welcome to the foothills of Alberta." I sit down across from them.

"Thanks," Olivia says with a quizzical look on her face as she studies the scars on mine.

"Abby has been my neighbor and best friend like forever," Simon says. He has a goofy smile on his face that I've never seen before. What's going on here?

"So you're one of those monster-home dwellers, too?" Olivia asks me as she throws her long, thick brown hair over her shoulder. I envy her curvy figure.

"Not me, I live in a run-down old farmhouse," I say.

"I can't believe how rich most everyone is at this school. Huge homes, designer clothes, top-of-the-line tech gadgets, almost everyone has their own car. So not what I'm used to coming from little old Greeley, Colorado." She talks with a slightly twangy accent.

"It probably seems that way," says Simon. "But a lot of students come from farming or ranching families. Not nearly as deep pockets as the oil executives and stockbrokers."

"Simon asked me to marry him in grade two." I blurt this out of nowhere, like a dog peeing to mark its territory. I'm such a loser.

"Oh really?" Olivia looks a little surprised that I hijacked the conversation but smiles at Simon. "How precocious of you."

"Yeah, but then I revoked the proposal, quickly realizing it would never work out between us," Simon says taking a gulp of coffee. Olivia giggles.

A girl about five years old comes up to our table and stares at me.

"Hi," I say.

She keeps staring. "What happened to your head?" she finally asks.

"I was attacked by a grizzly bear."

I look over at Olivia's expression and can't tell if she's shocked or amused. Has Simon been so distracted by this budding new friendship that he forgot to tell her the story of my disfigured face?

"Was it a big bear?" the little girl asks.

"Yup, really big. Huge, in fact. Especially her paws and mouth," I say. I hold up an opened hand like a big paw and try to open my mouth wide, but it doesn't have the effect I was hoping for. The girl looks at me blankly.

"I have a teddy bear named Cornelius," she says.

"Cornelius is a good name," I say. She checks out my face a little while longer and then runs to tell her mom.

"Sorry for prying, but a grizzly bear?" Olivia asks.

"True story," I say.

"I probably should have told her." Simon squirms, looking seriously uncomfortable.

"Are you kidding me?" Olivia says, looking from Simon to me.

"Not kidding," I say.

"Holy shit. I'm so sorry, Abby." Olivia covers her mouth.

"No need to apologize," I say.

"Wow," Olivia says. "I mean…wow. Like, are you doing okay?"

"I'm still alive to tell the tale, aren't I?"

"Any grizzly attacks I heard about in Colorado never turned out well," Olivia says.

Just then, Liam walks through the door. My heart gets all fluttery, and I have to take deep breaths to calm myself down. He greets Penny, who hands him my mocha and gestures to our table. His face falls into a gnarly pissed-off look, as if my being here has ruined his entire day. He brings my coffee and puts it on the table in front of me without acknowledging my presence. Bad customer service at the very least.

"Hey Liam," Simon says, "have you met Olivia?"

"I think you're in my chem class," Liam says.

"Yeah. Wasn't that exam today a joke? Nothing we learned about in class or in our textbooks," Olivia says and then takes a sip of her coffee.

"I know, right?" Liam says, glancing at me from the corner of his eye. "Well, better get to work. See you in class." He nods at Olivia.

"Yeah, see you, Liam," she says.

"Simon." He and Simon do the homie handshake.

"Bye," I say.

But he totally ignores me. Nice.

Liam stays hidden in the kitchen in the back of the café the whole time we're there. After about a half hour, I feel like a third wheel; Olivia and Simon clearly just want to talk. It all sounds geek to me.

"Are we still watching that Brazilian movie tonight?" I say to Simon as I stand to leave.

"Oh, sorry, I forgot. Olivia is going to come over and help me with my robotics project."

"Still needing help with that, eh?"

"Yeah, there's some programming I'm not familiar with."

"No worries, another time. Great meeting you, Olivia."

"You too, Abby," Olivia says. "See you around school."

As I walk to the door, Penny gives me another hug. "I think Liam misses you."

"Well if he does, he's sure got a strange way of showing it." I give her one of my crooked smiles. I turn and watch Simon so obviously smitten. I suddenly feel jealous, pissed off, and even more alone. I push open the door and leave.

***

After dinner, Dad goes up to bed early. I munch on popcorn as I watch another DVD of family movies. In the video, Jeannie and I act out a comedy improv/interpretive dance kind of thing. Jeannie's about ten, which makes me about eight. We have on our mom's long, flowing summer dresses that trail on the ground, and both of us wear a thick swish of sparkling-blue eye shadow and bright-red lipstick. Our performance is terrible, but the camera focuses on my mom, smiling, clapping, and laughing like we are the funniest, most talented people on the planet.

The next video shows a steep mountain trail with Mom hiking in the lead, then me, then Jeannie. Dad is pulling up the rear, videotaping. Other than a bit of wind, all you can hear is Jeannie complaining. "I'm so tired." "I didn't want to go hiking." "Why do you always make me come?" "I think I've got a blister on my toe." This makes me laugh out loud and almost choke on my popcorn. Typical Jeannie—never has taken to the great outdoors. Then I hear Mom say, "Derek, I told you this trail wasn't clearly marked. We should have gone on the other one." The camera then shows a panorama of snowy mountain peaks. Dad turns the camera on himself; he has an enormous goofy smile. I so miss that smile. In another video, I'm sitting at the kitchen table behind a birthday cake with ten candles. I look so dorky, like my teeth are way too big for my face. Mom, with her bald chemo head, sits right beside me at the table. After I blow out the candles, she wraps me in the biggest hug. I can now see the pain through her smile. She died two weeks later. I really needed her this past year. I really need her now.

I flop on my bed and wake up my laptop. I open my monologue doc and stare at the title page with only white screen underneath. What *do* I want to say? What is the story I want to tell? I look at the bear figurine on my bedside table for inspiration. I begin to outline a possible structure for the monologue, salvage a few paragraphs from my original draft that might fit. Piece those paragraphs together with a few phrases, then a few more. And then I can't stop writing. After almost two hours, I read it over, make some changes, and then email it to Owen. In my inbox is an email from Facing It. There's another meeting tomorrow night for teenagers. Topic: The Path to Unconditional Self-Acceptance. *Hmm...*

THE STORY IN MY BRAIN

Bio exam, last class of the day. I identify parts of the male reproductive system on a diagram: testicles, penis, scrotum, prostate, ejaculatory ducts, seminal vesicles. And for the female: ovaries, fallopian tubes, cervix, myometrium, uterus, vagina, labia majora, labia minora, Bartholin's glands, clitoris. I finish the exam but double-check my answers. Turns out I know my sex anatomy pretty well.

I look over at Liam, who is in deep concentration reading over his answers. Serena is right beside him, of course, doing the same. I remember the first time Liam and I had sex. Both of us were virgins (I never went very far with Mason), but we knew the mechanics of how it's all done. He touched my breasts and played with my nipples, which made me squirm and gave me goose bumps all over. Then we kissed on the lips. Touching tongues. It was so gentle at first, then so passionate and intimate. Liam then kissed my breasts, circled my nipples with his tongue. We began to touch and massage each other—clitoris, scrotum, vagina, penis. Liam got on top of me and slid his penis—

"Abby?" Mr. Jessop says, standing right at my desk. The whole class is looking at me, including Liam and Serena.

"What?" I'm now flushed—and incredibly horny. I try to pull my brain back.

Jessop holds out his hand. "Your exam. Time's up." I hand him my exam just as the bell rings.

Liam looks over at me. I wonder if he was remembering the same thing I was. By the look on his face, I truly doubt it.

***

Mr. Owen stops me in the hall outside the biology classroom. "Abby, I need a favor."

"Shoot."

"I'm trying to recruit some grade eight students from Strathcona Junior High to the drama program next year. I'm hoping you and Carter will run some improv activities with the group. It'll be an after-school thing."

"You sure you want me? I mean, you know..." If he's trying to recruit drama students, does he really want to risk my face scaring them away?

Owen looks at me with his no-nonsense face that used to unnerve me. "I wouldn't have asked you if I had any doubts, Abby. Yes or no."

"Okay, sure."

"I want them to meet a few grade twelve students who have been through the full high-school program. You may have to field some of their questions, too."

"Happy to help out," I say.

"Haven't confirmed a date, but I'll let you know. By the way, looking forward to reading the second draft of your monologue."

"I hope it's what you're looking for."

"Dig deep down to discover the heart of your story, Abby. Find the heart."

As I watch Owen leave, I think it's kind of brave of him asking me to represent his drama department. Grace walks toward me down the hall. I can tell by the look on her face that something is up.

***

At home, curled up on the couch in the family room, tears and snot stream down my face.

"I'm so sorry, Abbs." Grace sits beside me with her hand on my shoulder. She hands me a Kleenex. "But I thought it was best that you hear it from me."

"Yeah, way better than hearing it from Briar. I can imagine she's just dying to tell me." I wipe my face and blow my nose. Ruby whines beside me—she doesn't like it when anyone is sad. I pat her head to calm her down.

"Serena needed a date for grad, and Liam just happened to say yes. That's all."

"But Liam and I promised we'd go to grad together, no matter what," I say. Another gut-wrenching sob takes over my body. "I was sure he would keep his word."

"Maybe he just forgot. It was a long time ago. Besides, it's not serious with Serena or anything."

"Come on, Grace, it's obvious she's had her eyes on him for a while. I'm sure well before I came back to school."

"Maybe, but I doubt Liam is interested in anything more than a date for grad."

I imagine the photos of Liam, all handsome wearing a suit and tie, and Serena, looking her gorgeous self, plastered all over Instagram, Facebook, and Snapchat. I blow my nose again. "I totally deluded myself into thinking he was going to take me to grad. What was I thinking? He can barely look at me."

"He was on that backpacking trip, too, Abby. And he had his own run-in with the bear."

"I know. I can still hear him screaming."

"And he was so freaked out after seeing you in the hospital. Totally broken up by how badly you were injured. He kept telling me he was so worried you were going to die. I really thought he was losing it."

I guess I've never thought about it in quite that way before. I've been focused on myself and never really thought about how Liam might be dealing with his own trauma with the bear. But why won't he talk to me about it?

"What about you? Did Dax finally ask you to grad?" I say.

"Yeah, and I said no. Told him that I already had a date, which, of course, I don't."

"Oh, but you will soon enough." I blow my nose again.

"Having my doubts." Grace gives me a pleading look. "Why don't we go together, Abbs? We'd have such a blast."

"I'm sure we would, but no thanks." I want Grace to have the grad of her dreams—going with a guy, getting a corsage, drinking champagne on the limo ride with six other couples, staying up all night, drinking too much at the after-party, leaving with a different guy.

"Okay, but you're coming to the bush party with me next weekend."

"You're on." On the day of I'll tell her I have a terrible headache and can't go.

"I know what you're thinking, and I won't let you bail on me. I'll drag you out kicking and screaming if I have to."

Dear, sweet Grace.

"Remember how much fun we had last year?" I say.

"So awesome. Best year of my entire life."

"Hiking, backpacking, snowboarding…"

"Remember winter camping in Kananaskis?" Grace asks.

"You mean when it snowed like crazy overnight and we had to dig ourselves out of our tents?"

"And instead of snowshoeing, we spent the day building anatomically correct snowmen and women."

"The boobs on that one snow chick. I'm sure I still have a photo," I say.

"What about the enormous dick we sculpted on the snow stud? So big we had to prop it up with a tree branch." Grace and I crack up. The heaviness in my chest eases a bit.

"And remember the igloo Liam, Thomas, and Jarret made?" I say.

"Didn't we all squish in and sleep in there that night?"

"Yup, we did."

"Do you think you'll ever backpack again, Abbs?" Grace asks.

"I hope to one day, when I can build up my courage. You?"

Grace shrugs, gets all quiet. "You know, if my grandma hadn't been visiting from Ontario, I would have been on that trip with you and Liam."

"Yeah, I know."

"I keep wondering, if I had been with you guys, maybe…maybe somehow it wouldn't have happened," Grace says.

"But it did."

"Our trips to the mountains are some of my best memories." Grace looks at the mountain-scape painting hanging above the fireplace. "I don't know what happened this year. Things changed. For one, you weren't around, and Sarah, Jarret, and Thomas all moved away. Liam's pretty much kept to himself. Then I started to hang out with Serena more and more. And we know that the only way to get her outdoors is tanning on a beach in Mazatlán or Maui."

"True that."

Grace shakes her head. "Sometimes I don't like who I am anymore, or who I'm trying so desperately to be. I feel stuck in some weird movie. Can't take off the costume or the makeup. I wander around the same movie set with the same actors, see the same scenery, and there's only one script I can read from."

"I know exactly how you feel."

***

When I arrive in downtown Calgary at the Facing It workshop, Nadine is putting papers and pens on the tables. There are about six other teenagers here, and I recognize some of them from the first meeting. I make a point not to stare this time and smile at them instead. They all smile back. On a big whiteboard at the front of the room is a quote from the book *The Little Prince* by Antoine de Saint-Exupéry:

It is only with one's heart that one can see clearly.
What is essential is invisible to the eye.

"Welcome. Abby, is it?"

"Yeah, hi Nadine." I can't help but think she would be pretty if she didn't have that deep purple birthmark covering most of her face. But with her big smile and the way she talks and moves with such confidence, she seems like the perfect person to lead the workshop on self-acceptance. In fact, the more I watch her, the more I'm starting to think she's quite beautiful.

"Wondered if you'd be here tonight," Jade says as she sidles up beside me.

"Hey there. Surprised to see you. It didn't sound like you come to many of these meetings."

"Who doesn't need a little self-acceptance shot in the arm once in a while?"

"Can't argue with that," I say.

"Still wrestling your bear?"

"Guess you could say that."

"Could everyone please find a seat and we'll get started," Nadine says and moves to the front of the room. Jade and I sit at a table with a guy who has a web of thick scars that runs from his nose to his upper lip. This makes his front teeth stick out a bit.

"Hi, I'm Abby and this is Jade," I say to him, making sure I don't stare at the scar. Instead, I look right in his light-blue eyes.

"James." Slumped in his chair, he looks bored and uncomfortable—like he'd rather be anywhere but here.

Jade bends down and pretends to put something in her purse. "Cleft palate," she whispers. I'm pretty sure it's uncool to identify people by their condition, but it seems to be Jade's thing.

Nadine continues. "You'll see a questionnaire on the table in front of you that I'd like you to fill out before we begin. This is not like

Seventeen or *Cosmopolitan*, where you add up scores. In this quiz, there are no right or wrong answers. This is for you alone, and you don't have to share it with anyone unless you want to."

James twirls his pen and stares at the page, not even reading it.

I start my questionnaire.

- **Almost never**
- **Occasionally**
- **About half the time**
- **Fairly often**
- **Almost always**

When I look in the mirror, I like what I see, flaws and all.

- **Almost never**

When things are going badly for me, I see the difficulties as a part of life that everyone goes through.

- **About half the time**

When I think about my flaws, it tends to make me feel more separate and cut off from the rest of the world.

- **Almost always**

I believe that others would like me more if I looked different.

- **Fairly often**

I'm kind to myself when I'm having a difficult time.

- **~~Occasionally~~ Almost never**

I try to be understanding and patient toward those aspects of myself I don't like.

- **~~Occasionally~~ Almost never**

"Everybody finished?" Nadine asks. Nods around the room. James hasn't made one mark on the page. "Any insights, feelings, or comments you'd like to share?"

A girl with a clump of dyed black hair hanging over her face says, "Even when I know, without a doubt, that models in beauty magazines are airbrushed and Photoshopped, I still can't help but compare myself to this ridiculous ideal of what beauty is supposed to look like. I find it so hard to separate my facial disfigurement—I mean facial *difference*—from the real me."

"I can't believe how shitty I treat myself sometimes," Jade says. Others nod. "These questions kind of put things into perspective for me. I completely ignore the good things about myself. Who I really am deep down inside."

"Thanks for sharing that, Jade. Any others?"

I chime in. "I know I fixate and obsess on how unattractive I am—especially my face—and how beautiful all my friends are, and if only this hadn't happened to me, blah blah blah…" I start to choke up. "But I just don't know how to get out of this trap of self-sabotage, how to change the story going on inside my head."

"Hear! Hear!" Jade says.

"I can tell you from personal experience that changing that negative story in your head won't happen overnight," Nadine says. "And self-acceptance is a lifelong process for most people, facial differences or not. James, anything to add?"

James puts the pen down on the table. "Because of the way I look, I've gotten bullied as far back as I can remember. Beaten up, sworn at, spit on. Even pissed on. Twice I've tried to off myself. People like us," he gestures to everyone around the room, "haven't got a hope in hell of ever truly accepting ourselves because no one out in the world will ever accept us. So I think this little gathering here tonight is fucking bullshit and a total waste of my time." He stands and storms to the door.

Nadine smiles sadly as James leaves. "I understand where James is coming from all too well I'm afraid. Like many of you, I was born with a facial difference, and, like many of you, I have been bullied at times in my life. It's always incredibly hurtful and has, at times, totally shattered my self-esteem and self-confidence. But my big life lesson has been that until I truly accept myself with all my flaws, inside and out, how can I expect anyone else to accept me?"

Nadine's words hit home; I feel terrified and hopeful at the same time.

"Can I add just one thing?" Jade says. "Lately, I've started a gratitude journal. Sounds flaky, I know, but every day I try to write down at least one thing I'm grateful for. It's really helped me get—sorry for being gross—my head out of my ass and see that there's lots to be thankful for, even with this." Jade points at the burn scars on her face.

"Great idea, Jade," Nadine says. "Anyone else write down their thoughts of gratitude?" A few nods around the room. "That's all for tonight, but I hope to see you all back for part two of this workshop in which we'll discuss the practice of self-acceptance."

The energy in the room feels lighter somehow, like more oxygen was pumped into the air. More people are holding their heads up a little higher, looking one another in the eyes. More smiles, more laughter.

Before I leave the room, I take one more look at the quote written on the board.

It is only with one's heart that one can see clearly.
What is essential is invisible to the eye.

Jade and I chat as we leave the building and walk down the street toward the parking lot.

"Couldn't help but think tonight that if I'd hurt anyone in my car crash, there wouldn't be a hope in hell of self-acceptance," Jade says. "How could anyone carry around that guilt?"

"So you were alone?"

She nods. "After getting shit-faced at a party in Cochrane, I drove my car off the road, rolled, then crashed in the ditch." She hunts for her keys in her purse. "That's how the fire started. A hunky firefighter dragged me out of my car before I became a total crispy critter. Guess I'm lucky that only one side of my body got fried."

"No other cars involved?"

"Nope, thank God, or my license would have been suspended for way more than a year. The judge could have sentenced me to jail for the DUI. I think she took pity on me knowing my life would never be the same. A year without driving wasn't so bad."

When we get to Jade's car she says, "You talked about trying to change the story going on in your head. I can totally relate. For what it's worth, when I bad-mouth myself, I visualize lassoing all my negative thoughts and rounding them up. And then I imagine letting a stampede of positive thoughts out of an enormous corral."

"Obviously a Calgary Stampede girl."

"You got it." Jade smiles. "All I'm saying, Abby, is if you nip the self-trashing in the bud, change those negative thoughts into something positive about yourself, you might notice life get a little brighter."

"Makes sense. Thanks."

"Oh, and check out a Facebook page called 'Evolve.' A bit touchy-feely, but it's a good reminder that all us humans are in this together. See you later."

Jade gets in her car, starts it, and drives away.

EVOLVING

When I get home from the Facing It meeting, Dad is at the kitchen table, this time with a grin on his face as he types something on his laptop. I text Jeannie.

Well, I nevah! I think pops might be setting up his first online date
No way-ask him!

"What's up, Dad?"

"What do you mean?"

"You've got a funny look on your face."

Dad looks right at me with that same funny look. "Okay," he says with a chuckle, "a woman contacted me. Through the dating site."

"Do tell. Who is she?"

I was right
Ask who she is
I did already

"Her name is Belinda."

Belinda
What else?

"Tell me more," I say.

"She's around my age, she's an accountant with an oil company, has a daughter."

Around dad's age, accountant, has a daughter

Belinda the accountant? Hmm...and...

"And?"

"And that's all I'm telling you," Dad says with that same look and closes his laptop.

What's she look like?

He closed his laptop on me-that's all I got

Is he at least meeting her?

"Aren't you going to meet her for the requisite first coffee date?" I ask.

"What are you, the grand inquisitor?"

"Yup."

So?????

"I'm heading upstairs to finish my book. Have a good sleep, kiddo."

He won't tell

Ruby follows me to my room, jumps up on my bed, and curls up. I look at myself closely in the mirror—the scars on my face, my non-existent left cheek, my crooked mouth. I use a hand mirror to look at the back of my head where my hair has finally grown in enough to cover the scars on my scalp. Something to be thankful for, something to put in a gratitude journal. If I had one. I take off my T-shirt and run my fingers over the thick scars on my chest. I have a flashback of the bear's gigantic paw swiping at me. I hold my bear figurine tightly in my hand before I get ready for bed.

I open my laptop and check Facebook. Not surprisingly, there's another message from UR SO FN UGLY: "You're so ugly that when you look in the mirror your reflection throws up." I glance up and see my face in my dresser mirror. A tidal wave of negative thoughts and feelings about myself flood my mind: *I am so fucking ugly. No wonder Liam can barely look at me. I'm not fit for public viewing. I don't deserve friends.*

I immediately put the brakes on those thoughts and search Facebook for "Evolve." It's basically photos with captions or quotes. I get what Jade said about it being touchy-feely. I scroll through several quotes. One really resonates: *You teach people how to treat you by what you allow, what you stop, and what you reinforce.*

I grab my phone.

"How do I block someone from Messenger?" I ask Siri in a quivery voice.

Siri provides a list of websites. I scroll through, find one, and follow the instructions. Done! No more UR SO FN UGLY. I feel hopeful somehow. Why didn't I do this sooner? In some warped way, do I think I deserve to be bullied after what I did to Mason?

"Siri, how do I delete Facebook?" Another list of sites to show me how. But I decide not to. At least not yet.

I open the bedside-table drawer and reach down to take out my research notebook stuffed with printed-off photos of grizzly bears. I touch the notebook cover with my fingertips but don't pick it up. Close the drawer, instead.

I go to my dresser mirror and examine every square inch of my face. I'm not to blame for what happened to me. It was just an unfortunate situation of being in the wrong place at the wrong time. The criss-crossing scars. Concave cheek. Right eye mostly hidden under the lid. Scrunched up forehead. All of these things are just the covering, a mask. This face isn't me. It's not who I really am—it's what I wear.

***

I'm super-nervous as Mr. Owen hands out the second drafts of the plays and monologues to the class. He finally comes to me, hesitates, and hands me the manuscript. On it says:

This is still a very rough draft; you've barely touched the surface of what your story could be. Where's the real drama in your story? Where's the pulse? Where's the anguish? Where is the heart? Your monologue needs much more work to become a polished draft.
J. Owen

I feel like I've been punched in the stomach. I worked so hard on this draft, was sure it was so much better. I'm starting to wonder if I have it in me. Suddenly, the realization that I'll actually have to perform my monologue in front of the class, maybe even the whole school and community, scares the shit out of me. Mine is not a light-hearted comedy about a teenager coming to terms with saying good-bye to an imaginary friend. Like Tammy's, my monologue is about a real-life, gut-wrenching event that has changed my life forever.

"Next up is Mason and Dax with their one-act play titled *Therapy for a Superhero.*" Mason, wearing a bright blue T-shirt with the Superman logo, and Dax stroll to the front of the class. They both have stupid grins. The old, worn-out, gold couch with swirly patterns that's usually at the back of the class has been moved to the front. Mason lies down on it, and Dax sits in a chair holding a pen and a notebook.

"You gotta help me, doc. I'm sure someone is spiking my beer with kryptonite," Mason says.

"Tell me why you feel this way," Dax says. The two look at each other and crack up.

"Gentlemen, focus, please," Owen says.

They keep laughing for another minute, which makes some people in the class start laughing. But not me.

"First of all, when I tried to stop a semi truck from hitting an old lady crossing the street, I got this scratch." Mason points to a spot on his arm. "And I used to be able to leap tall buildings in a single bound, but now it takes me, like, two or three tries. And don't even get me started about my superhuman speed. Usain Bolt could kick my butt in a race."

Dax writes in his notebook. "How long have you been having these paranoid delusions?"

"Well, it all started when I was having a beer with my peeps, you know, Batman, Robin, Wonder Woman, Spider-Man…"

Their play is lame. Really lame. At least I don't have to worry about them being competition for the Theater on the Edge internship. I can't help but wonder if all bullies feel like someone put kryptonite in their beer. That they're compensating somehow, because deep down they feel powerless. Powerless like me.

***

I watch Dax and Mason leave the class and wait as long as I can before I leave. Finally, I head for the stairs. My heart races and my stomach is full of anxious butterflies when I see them and a few other guys on the landing. I breathe deeply several times. *I'm OK just as I am. I'm confident. I have control over my thoughts, feelings, and choices. I can stand up for myself.*

"Bear Bait, where have you been all my life?" Mason says as he watches me slowly walk down the stairs.

"She's been in Uglyville, where else?" says one guy, which makes them all laugh their asses off.

My knees are wobbly and my stomach flip-flops as I walk right up to Mason. A foot taller than me, I look up at his face. "You and your stoner posse need to stop. This is not okay. And I know this might be a shock to you, but you're actually not that funny." The guys say "Whoa" and crack up. "What you're doing to me is hurtful, and I want you to stop."

"Stop? Is that what you said, Bear Bait? Or should I say slut? You want us to stop?" Mason bends down and looks me right in the eye. "Oh, but we've barely even started yet."

He stays right in my face. His breath smells like pot smoke and sauerkraut.

"I'll do whatever it takes to make you stop this. I'll go to the police if I have to." I hope that didn't sound like the empty threat that it is. I elbow him hard, squeeze past him, and race down the stairs.

FASHIONISTAS

Tammy and I make our way through West Ridge Mall.

"There are a few boutiques in here that I think you'll like. But first, we're getting our makeup done," Tammy says.

"What?"

"I phoned ahead. They can take both of us." Tammy strolls up to a small kiosk with rows of mascara and colorful eye shadow and lipstick.

"How about I just watch you," I say.

"No way. As your extreme makeover consultant, I insist we start here," Tammy says. "No discussion. End of story."

When the two girls working at the New Self counter look at Tammy and then at me, they share a wide-eyed, uncomfortable look. Tammy and I are obviously going to be the biggest challenges of their aesthetics careers.

"I'm Tammy."

"Oh." She looks at Tammy in a weird way. "I'm Jane and this is Savannah. We'll be doing your makeup today."

"Let's get started, shall we? This might take a while," Tammy says, winking at me.

I get Savannah. She has pink hair the color of cotton candy, but her makeup looks natural, even tasteful, as far as makeup goes. "You can sit here." She gestures to a stool. "Do you want to pick colors for your eye shadow and lipstick?"

"I'll just have what you're wearing. All of it," I say, feeling incredibly self-conscious as she inspects every inch of my face, probably trying to figure out how the hell she's going to cover up the disaster. Oops. Replace that with a positive thought. Savannah is probably trying to figure out how to maximize my best features.

"I'm an Ivory 2 foundation, but I'm thinking the Beige 3 concealer will work best with your skin color," she says.

Concealer. Good luck, Savannah. I catch myself again. No negative thoughts. No trashing myself. I try to reboot my brain again for a sunnier point of view. I look over at Jane, who is applying foundation to Tammy's face. There's a long patch of whiskers that didn't get shaved.

"Sorry about the racing stripes," Tammy says. "My blade is pretty dull."

"When do you usually shave?" Jane asks.

"As soon as I get out of bed. Facial hair is the bane of my existence."

"First thing in the morning, the skin is puffy from sleep," Jane says. "Try waiting about twenty to thirty minutes for your skin to tighten back up to normal. You'll get a closer shave because more of the hair follicle is exposed."

"Well, aren't you just a fountain of knowledge," Tammy says with a big smile.

When my makeover is done, I look at myself in the mirror in total disbelief. The way Savannah concealed, toned, and blushed my face, I look almost normal—at least as normal as I've looked in nearly a year. I'm still wearing a mask, but I like this one better.

"I don't want to give you the heavy sales pitch," Savannah says, "but I think if you invest in anything, the concealer and blush would be your best bet."

"I can only afford one, so how about the concealer," I say. I look over at Tammy's dramatic sapphire-blue eye shadow and bright red lipstick.

"Can you please take our picture?" Tammy hands Jane her cell phone. I try on my best smile.

I have to say, Tammy and I both look pretty darn good.

After we pay for our new makeup, Tammy leads me into Bella's, a woman's clothing store. I remember shopping here with Grace and Serena a few years ago, when I cared a whole lot more about what I wore. I bought one of my favorite summer dresses here.

A salesgirl who looks even younger than me approaches. "Anything I can help with?" I notice she curiously studies my face but doesn't give me the usual shocked or appalled look that I expect when in public. Could it be the makeup?

"We're looking for dresses," Tammy says.

"Follow me," she says and leads us to the rack. "Let me know if you have any questions about sizes or anything."

Tammy and I start looking.

"What about this?" Tammy holds up a bright, flowery dress.

"Nah, not my style."

I look through the short cotton dresses. I catch a glimpse of myself in the large mirror on the wall. Definitely don't look like the old me, but maybe this is the new me? Even my crooked smile looks kind of cute. A positive thought about myself right off the bat. Yay me!

Tammy and I go into the change room area and each try on a pile of dresses. Most of the ones Tammy wanted me to try on were definitely not me. Except one—a short, sleeveless navy-blue cotton sundress with a high neckline that covers my chest scars. It has an embroidered pattern on the top, with a thin, matching line of embroidery along the bottom. The same pattern also outlines two small pockets. I look at my reflection in the mirror. I like what I see. And I've got just enough money left to buy it.

"Abby, you in here?" Tammy's outside my door.

"Yup." I open my small cubicle door. She's wearing the bright, floral-patterned dress.

"Wow, awesome dress," Tammy says, looking me up and down. "I knew that one would work for you. You look hot, lady."

"Thanks. I was thinking the very same thing." I turn and look at the back of the dress. "And speaking of hot—look at you. That dress looks so good on you."

Tammy examines herself from all angles in the full-length mirror.

"I do look good, don't I?" she says with an enormous smile that would light up a dark room.

We stand in front of the change room mirror for a long while staring at ourselves. Both broken, raw, traumatized in our own way, but desperate to rebuild ourselves outside and in. My chest is all light and fluttery.

***

When I drive up to the house, Dad's just leaving. He's showered, shaved, and changed out of his work clothes and into khakis and a nice navy V-neck sweater.

I roll down my window. "What's shaking?"

"Just heading out."

"Where are you off to?" As if I don't know. And obviously Dad knows that I know.

"Okay, Curious George, I'm going on a coffee date."

"Well, look at you, wasting no time at all."

Dad smiles, taps on the hood of my car. "See you later, kiddo," he says as he walks to his newly washed truck.

"Are you meeting Belinda the accountant?" I call out. He waves but doesn't turn around.

OVER THE EDGE

Grace sleeps with her head on my shoulder as the school bus drives down Highway 1 through the rolling foothills toward the mountains. The combined guys' and girls' phys ed classes are taking the morning to hike Mount Yamnuska, one of the first mountains when heading west toward Banff, about a forty-minute drive from Springbank. A pretty easy hike my family has done together a few times. I look out the window at the early morning sun lighting up the still-snowy peaks. The sky is bright blue, only a few wispy brushstrokes of white clouds.

This will be my first hike, my first time in the wilderness in ten months and fourteen days. But who's counting? I had to give myself a good talking to this morning when I woke up. Looked myself right in the mirror (wearing my new concealer, of course) and told myself that I'm brave and courageous and strong. I vowed to think only positive, happy thoughts. But as insurance, I went on the Parks Canada website to read the "Weekly Bear Report." Grizzly bears sighted at Taylor Creek, Moraine Creek, Bow Lake, Baker Creek, the Sawback, Lake Louise ski area, Num-Ti-Jah Lodge, and the Banff Springs Golf

Course. No bears sighted near Yamnuska. Besides, even if there was a bear in the area, it wouldn't come near a big group of hikers. But that's what I thought last time.

I look around the bus. A few seats ahead, Briar sits with Keegan, and across the aisle, Serena is with Liam. She's chatting his ear off while he nods, looking out the window. I wonder if this is his first time in the great outdoors since our fateful hike. Something to put in my gratitude journal, if I had one, is that Mason and Dax are skipping the hike.

Mr. Harris and Ms. Wong stand. "Quiet for a second everyone," Ms. Wong says. Grace lifts her head and opens her eyes. "Yamnuska is an Indigenous name that translates to wall of stone. Yamnuska comes from the Stoney Nakoda word *lyamnathka*, which means steep cliffs or flat-faced mountain. And if you look out the window," she points to the north, "you'll see that's a great description."

"But there's not going to be any rock scrambling today. Right, Keegan?" Mr. Harris says.

"What? No scrambling?" Keegan says jokingly. Briar lets out a loud, forced laugh.

"Right, Liam?" says Mr. Harris. Liam smiles and nods.

"I want everyone to stay on the well-marked path," Ms. Wong says. "We'll have a rest at the top. But don't worry, folks, we'll have you back for third period this afternoon." Groans from around the bus.

The bus pulls into the parking lot at the trailhead. Everyone grabs their day pack and files out of the bus. Grace stands and throws her pack over her shoulder.

"That mountain's not going to hike itself," she says with a big smile and then takes a swig from her water bottle. She stuffs her thick black curls under a baseball cap.

I'm frozen in my seat but somehow finally manage to stand and head down the aisle. The bus driver has already plugged earbuds into his phone and is listening to music, while he plays a video game on his iPad.

The group huddles around the teachers. "As I said, stay on the path and stick together. Okay, let's get moving," Mr. Harris says. The keeners lead the way. I used to be one of those keeners.

"I'm surprised Serena even came," Grace says. "She doesn't walk any more than she has to—she even drives around the parking lot at the mall forever just to get a spot close to the door."

"I have a feeling Liam has something to do with it," I say.

"I think you might be right. How are you feeling about, you know...?" She gestures toward Liam and Serena.

I shrug. "Heartbroken and numb at the same time, if that makes any sense."

"Strangely, it kind of does."

Ms. Wong walks up to us. "How are you doing, Abby? Is your leg feeling strong?"

Grace starts up the trail.

"Just great." I put on my happy face. I'm strong. I'm courageous. I'm...I'm...seriously anxious.

"Excellent," she says. "I'm glad you came." She joins the line of hikers just ahead.

I slip on my pack and catch up to Grace, who's waiting for me. Liam, who's a little bit ahead, glances back. When he sees me, he turns around and keeps walking. He looks strong, buff, like he's been working out.

Grace must sense my hesitation because she links my arm in hers.

"Let's not be the stragglers," she says. I look behind us. There are still a few people near the bus, tightening up boots and eating granola bars. "We so used to kick ass on the trail."

"Yeah, we sure did." Did being the operative word.

Grace hangs on to me for a while, but the trail narrows and we have to go single file. Being in the mountains again feels surreal, like I'm floating above my body, and I can barely feel my hiking boots touch the ground. I can't tell yet whether it's a good or bad feeling. After a while, my bad leg starts to ache. I stretch, but the ache doesn't go away.

The trail narrows by a steep rock face. I look down over the edge at the field below and see a large brown shape in a grove of trees. I shake my head, blink a few times, and look again. The brown mass is now moving.

"Bear," I say to Grace, pointing down the cliff.

"No way," she says, peering down through the trees. "It's just a moose."

"Trust me, it's a bear. A brown bear."

Even though the bear is about 100 feet down a cliff from me, my knees buckle, my whole body starts to wobble. Sweat beads above my top lip. I look over the edge again and see the bear paw at the ground, digging up roots.

"Holy shit, I think it is a bear," Grace says, studying my face. "You okay?"

"Yeah, I think so." I start back on the trail with Grace close behind. I begin to feel dizzy, especially looking down the rock face at the bear. My eyes dart around as we hike through a grove of trees. I hike like that for about ten minutes. I stop. Close my eyes. All I can see is the grizzly barreling toward me, growling, mouth open wide, razor teeth bared. I sink down, the sharp rocks poking into my bare knees. "I can't do this," I say to Grace. "I just can't."

A few others hiking behind us ask what's wrong. I cover my face with my hands and close my eyes.

"Tell Wong and Harris we're heading back to the bus," Grace says and then squats down beside me. She puts her hand on my back, which helps calm the shaking. We stay like this for what seems like an hour, but it's probably only a few minutes.

I open my eyes and stare at the pebbles on the trail. Lift my head and slowly stand up. I feel like I'm going to puke, but nothing comes. Grace holds my elbow and guides me back down the trail.

***

Simon plops a huge scoop of caramel hazelnut fudge fantasy ice cream into his already overflowing bowl. We've just finished watching a Japanese blood-and-guts yakuza film.

"I'm such a loser," I say, sticking my spoon into a glob of caramel.

"Hey, go easy on yourself." He puts the top on the ice-cream carton. The kitchen is so large, when the freezer door closes, there's a loud echo. "I freaked seeing that bear behind bars at the zoo, and I've never even been attacked."

"I thought I was ready."

"It's not as if you were faking it to get off class or anything."

"Speaking of getting off, anything happening yet with you and Olivia?"

"You're shameless." He spoons a big hunk of ice cream into his mouth.

"Come on, tell me. You know you want to," I tease.

He sighs, thinks for a bit. "Well…we made out the other night."

"How was it?"

He blushes, looks down into his bowl. "Awkward. Weird. Nice."

"See, didn't I tell you?"

"But there's a problem." He puts his spoon down. "Olivia isn't a virgin and I am."

"And the problem is…?"

"The problem is I don't know what the hell I'm doing. I know sex is supposed to be all natural and everything, but…"

"Is Olivia pressuring you to have sex?"

"Of course not."

"So you feel ready?"

"Yes, I'm ready. At least I think I am."

"Then all you really have to know is what gets put where."

"Don't be so crass." He looks serious. "This is important. I want this first experience with Olivia to be memorable. For both of us."

"Just take it slow then. Liam and I didn't have sex the very first time we got naked together. It wasn't until the third or fourth time. We just…explored for a while."

"But what if I chicken out at the last minute? Or if things…don't work the way they're supposed to."

"That should be absolutely okay. If Olivia doesn't understand, say adios."

"What if we actually do it and I make a fool of myself?"

"Not that I have a ton of experience to go on here, but I do know that it can be awkward at first. Just try to relax, experiment, enjoy. And wear a condom."

"Yes, Mother."

We're quiet for a while as we both scrape the bottom of our bowls.

Simon looks up with a terrified look in his eyes. "What happens if she wants oral sex?"

"One step at a time, big guy."

***

I hear Dad open the kitchen door. He's home late.

"Were you out with Belinda the accountant again tonight?"

"No." Dad sits on a chair and unties his work boots.

"How was your coffee date with her yesterday?"

"It was fine." Dad pulls off one boot at a time.

"Just fine? What's she like? Are you going to see her again?"

"So, every time I have a date I'll get the third degree?"

"Pretty much. Spill it, Dad."

"Okay, she seemed nice."

"Just nice? Is she pretty?"

Dad takes off his jacket and throws it over a chair. "Well, she wasn't the same person portrayed in her profile photo."

"She posted someone else's picture?!"

"No, but it was a photo of her about twenty years ago—when she was about forty pounds lighter. I don't understand why anyone would misrepresent themselves like that."

"Hellooo—she's trying to meet a man."

"I would have met her as she is, but the deception is a big turnoff." Dad opens the fridge.

"Yeah, but you're a nice guy. It's all about how you look, Dad. Trust me. Most men wouldn't give an overweight middle-aged woman the time of day, no matter how nice or intelligent or interesting she is."

"I don't think online dating is for me." Dad pulls a plate of leftovers out of the fridge.

"You've only gone on one date. You've got to give it some time."

"My email box is full, and I just don't have the energy for it."

"That's because you're such a great catch. Let me help. I'll sort potential dates for you," I say.

"Thanks, but no." Dad puts the plate in the microwave.

"Dad, please don't quit. Not just yet."

DÉJÀ VU ALL OVER AGAIN

Dance music blares in the drama room. "Welcome to Improv-a-ganza!" I say as I dance and Carter moonwalks around the room in front of a pack of grade eight students. Some get into it and dance along with us, some watch us mildly amused, others have crossed arms and a too-cool-for-school look. Or at least too cool for our little improv class. Carter turns down the volume.

"How many of you have ever done improv?" I ask. "How many have seen improv performed?" Two or three nod.

"Improv is the art of making things up on the spot," I say, projecting my voice, my head held high. Although a few of the students did a double take when they first saw me, no one is gawking, which has given me a little more oomph. At least I can *act* confident in front of an audience.

"Improv is acting without a script," says Carter, bouncing around like a boxer. He hasn't kept still the whole time; maybe he's nervous. I feel strangely calm for a change.

"Before we start, you'll need to know some basic guidelines," I say. "In improv, we want to avoid what's called Blocking. Blocking is when one person says something and the other person replies with a statement that directly contradicts what the first person says. Here's an example."

Carter faces me and says in a robot-like voice, "I'm from planet Xostarvis in the Drizon galaxy."

"No, you're not. You're Carter from Springbank, Alberta, Canada, planet Earth in the Milky Way galaxy," I say. Carter, head down, sulks and walks away. Chuckles around the room. I turn to the group, "As you can see, blocking is death to an improv scene."

Carter says, "However ridiculous the statement one person says, the other has to go along with it. This is called Agreement or Yes, and…here's an example." He stands straight with one arm at his side and the other hand raised in a salute. I stand with hands on hips, head back, trying to look like a model.

"It's tough being made of wax," Carter says to me.

"Yeah, and it sure doesn't help that we're in hell," I say.

"I'm melting," Carter says in a high-pitched voice, and we slowly "melt" to the floor. A few more laughs from the group.

"Before we divide you into groups, in the true spirit of improv, we'll let you tell us a scenario to act out. Anybody?"

"Choosing a gift for your boyfriend," one girl shouts out.

Carter and I face each other.

"Can I help you?" Carter says with a sophisticated British accent.

"Yeah, well, I just don't know," I reply, acting like a ditz, pretending I'm chewing gum. "My boyfriend is so hard to buy for."

"Tell me what your boyfriend is like."

"He's *sooo* freakin' hot." Laughs from the group. "And he has a big-ass Jeep with monster wheels about a mile high. And—"

"But what are his interests?" Carter asks.

"Interests? Well, he loves ultimate fighting, especially when there's blood." I act like I'm kickboxing. "Lots of blood." I punch the air a few more times.

"Hmm, anything else you can tell me about him?"

"He loves shootin' stuff, you know, like cans and bottles off fence posts. Rats and rabbits." My hand is the gun. I aim. "*Pow-pow-pow.*"

"After careful consideration, may I recommend an exquisite shirt, tie, and cufflink set," Carter says.

"Aces, man." I give him the thumbs-up. "Jethro will love 'em."

Carter and I bow and everyone claps.

"Thanks everyone. Remember, there are no mistakes in improv, only opportunities," I say. "Divide yourselves into groups of four. We'll start with a few warm-up games."

***

Every single grade eight student, even the ones who came in with attitude and crossed arms, thanks Carter and me for a great workshop. Many stay around to ask questions about the drama program. Mission accomplished.

"I couldn't have done this without you, Abby," Carter says when they've all left.

"You would have been fine."

"No way. You had this group under some weird I'll-do-anything-you-ask-me-to spell. I don't know how you did it."

"Aw, shucks," I say, feeling kind of chuffed.

"I probably would have lost it on that one kid. What a little shit."

"He wasn't so bad. Just a bit hyper, that's all."

"Have you ever thought about becoming a teacher, if and when you grow up?" Carter says, and I give him a playful jab in the ribs.

"Never even crossed my mind."

***

"The University of Calgary website says I can do a concurrent degree in Education and Drama," I tell Jeannie on my cell phone as I scroll on my laptop.

"That would be so perfect for you, Bean," Jeannie says. "But I'm checking UBC—I want you in Vancouver with me. If you get your application in for this fall, we could even find a place together."

"Whoa, put on the brakes, speedy. I have at least one more surgery this summer, which will probably snowball into more. Remember the drill? No idea when I'll be ready for university, but based on my last recovery, it won't be this fall, that's for sure."

"Well, if I get accepted to med school, I'll be in university for about a decade, so there will be plenty of time to make plans."

A text bloops.

"Just got a text from Grace. I should say good-bye."

"Go to the party tonight for crying out loud. Have fun. You deserve it."

The bush party is at an old campground by a creek off Highway 22. Part of me wants to bail, and part of me wants to put on some concealer and get the heck out of the house for a change.

Tell me you're coming tonight

Maybe

No maybe. No way

Okay, then I'll be DD

No way-got my mom's car–I want u 2 have fun tonight
You know I've never been much of a drinker
Tonight would be a good night to start-u got lots of catching up to do
Nope. Remember the words of every self-respecting partier-don't waste a good party when you've got a willing DD
U sure?
Yup
K, see u later!!!!!

***

Cows hang their heads over the barbwire fence, munching on grass. I guess the grass *is* greener on the other side. They moo at us as we turn off the highway and drive down a long, bumpy road through the thick bush. The sun is almost touching the mountains on the horizon. Music thumps through the trees as we get closer.

"Sounds like the party started without us," Grace says.

My first party in about a year and I feel as jittery as I did on my first day back at school. At the end of the road are dozens of cars. The whereabouts of the party probably got texted, tweeted, and Facebook-messaged to friends and friends of friends. I see Mason's truck. My heart hammers against my ribs. In my mind, I repeat my new mantra over and over: *I am strong. I am courageous. I am confident. I have my own kind of beauty. I am worthy.* I look around for Liam's mom's car, but it isn't here. Not sure if I feel relieved or disappointed.

When we walk toward the roaring fire in the large fire pit, the techno music hits me like a slap—throbbing bass and the synth that sounds like a buzz saw. I hate techno. Except for all the people I don't know, this party is like déjà vu. The rugby jocks—Brandon, Keegan, Devin, and Miles—and a rowdy crowd of other guys whoop and holler it up playing drinking games at picnic tables. No Liam.

Grace and I squeeze through a group of people where Serena and Briar are drinking bottled Caesars. On the other side of the fire I see Mason, Dax, the posse, and a bunch of others pounding back beer. I haven't missed a thing this past year—the usual suspects doing their usual things. I walk around the fire and get as close to them as I can without being noticed. I pull out my phone and take photos of them—one of the posse opening a bag of pot, another one rolling a joint, Dax passing a joint to Mason, Mason taking a toke. With the fire close by, the photos come out pretty well. I walk back to where Grace is.

"Hey, bitches," Briar says in a loud Caesar-induced voice and throws her arms around both of us. I can smell the alcohol and spicy Clamato juice on her breath. Not pleasant.

I wave at Serena. She gives me a half-hearted smile.

"Want one?" Briar holds up her drink.

"No need," says Grace, pulling two bottles of cider out of her purse. "My mom donated this to the cause."

"Abby? How about a Caesar, or should I say, seizure?" Briar asks.

"Had enough seizures in my day, but thanks. I'm driving." I reach into my purse for an organic mango and orange juice.

"Your mom is so cool," Serena says to Grace. Serena is weaving and having trouble focusing—she's obviously downed a few "seizures" already.

"She's just practical. She knows I won't drink and drive, and if I'm not driving and going to a party, she knows I'm going to drink. So I tell her if she gives me two bottles, I'll stop there." Grace opens one of the ciders.

"But do you always stop at two?" Serena asks.

Grace says, "Well…usually."

"What about the party at Liam's cabin last fall?" Briar says. "Don't think you stopped at two that night. Never seen someone barf so much in my whole life." Briar lets out her loud, obnoxious drunken laugh.

Grace never told me about Liam's party.

"Yes, well, remind me never to play beer pong with the basketball team," Grace says.

"Even if I was legal, my mother would probably still lecture me about drinking." Serena slurs her words then guzzles the rest of her drink. "But it's not about me getting drunk and maybe getting pregnant or dying in a car crash. It's all about me getting fat from alcohol."

"Seriously?" I say.

"Yup, that's my mom for you." Serena twists the top off another bottle. "Sure has her motherly priorities in the right place, doesn't she?" Takes a big gulp. Burps. Hiccups.

Dax and Mason muscle their way through the crowd. Mason pounds his chest and lets out an intoxicated Tarzan yell to announce himself. When Dax sees me, he elbows Mason. I put my juice down on a picnic table to stop it from spilling out of my shaking hands. *Steady, girl*, I say to my pounding heart. Even though my face feels tense, even more crooked than usual, I smile at them. Hold my shaking hands so tightly, my nails dig into my skin.

"Better watch how much you drink tonight," Mason says to me. "Wouldn't want you to get off balance or anything." Dax snorts.

I hold up my juice. "Doubt that's going to happen." It comes out sounding so lame. Grace gives me a questioning look. I shrug.

Mason slams into me, almost knocks me to the ground. My juice spills all over me.

"Don't be such an asshole, Mason," Grace says. Mason gives her a goofy smile, and he and Dax join the drinking gamers. Briar and Serena follow.

"Want to join the crazies?" Grace asks.

"I think I'll just hang here for a while," I say. "I'll be there soon." Grace nods and follows the rest. I find a used Kleenex in my pocket and try unsuccessfully to mop up the juice on my jacket and jeans.

I walk away down a long path to drown out at least some of the thumping music. I come to a clearing and climb on top of a picnic table. The night air is cool and fresh, the sky sprinkled with stars. Why did I even come to this party? I feel like a poser trying to fit in with Serena, Briar, and Grace. It's so clear none of us are the same people we were a year ago. Especially me. So why am I even trying?

Rowdy voices echo down the path. Mason, Dax, and others appear through the trees.

"It's Bear Bait," Dax says, pointing at me.

Oh my God, oh my God! I want to jump down from the picnic table and run as fast as I can, but my whole body is frozen in place, too terrified to budge. As they come closer, I rummage in my purse to find my phone. Shit, where is it?

In about a nanosecond, Mason is right in my face. The smell of beer and pot on his breath makes me want to barf.

"Who invited you to this party? Huh, Abby? My invitation said no sluts allowed," says Mason. "Yours, too?" He looks over at Dax.

"Yup, mine, too," Dax says.

I finally have my hand on my phone. I peer down into my purse and type in my passcode.

"Hey guys," Mason says to his friends. "Abby and I need a little privacy to, you know, get reacquainted."

Dax snorts as he and the others slowly head back down the path toward the bonfire. I search for Grace's contact. Mason reaches over me. I struggle as he digs his hand into my purse and snatches my phone.

"Give it back, Mason." I swipe at the air as he easily holds me back with one hand while searching my phone with his other.

"Let's see who you've been texting." I keep fighting to reach for my phone as he scrolls through my texts. "Your father…your grandmother…your sister…Grace. That's it? One friend? Fuckin' pitiful if you ask me. I'd say this is a waste of a good iPhone." He launches my phone far into a thick grove of trees.

"You're such an asshole," I yell. I climb off the picnic table and start toward the trees to find my phone. Mason grabs my arm and pulls me closer to him. I try to wriggle out of his grip, but his hand is like a shackle.

"You kept saying no to me and then went slutting around behind my back, didn't ya? No girl does that to me without serious payback."

"Leave me alone!" I try to pull away from him, but he twists my arm and it feels like it's going to snap. The rage inside me burns and builds.

"You're not going to say no to me now, Abby. But it'd be *way* better for me if there was a bag over your fucking-ugly face."

I fight to get out of his grip. Swing my good leg as hard as I can and kick Mason in the crotch. My foot hurts like hell. He drops to the ground. Moaning. Calling me a fucking bitch. I run towards the path—right into Liam.

"Get him away from me," I say to Liam, my voice shaking.

"What the hell's going on?" Liam looks from me to Mason, who is now standing.

"That little bitch just kicked me in the balls," Mason says.

"Only after you tried to assault me," I say in as loud and confident a voice as I can. "In case you've never heard, no means no, Mason!" My whole body is trembling. I lean up against Liam to steady myself.

"This isn't over," Mason says, with hatred in his eyes. "Not by a long shot."

"Get lost," Liam says to Mason.

"Go fuck yourself, Liam. Because I doubt you'll ever want to fuck her again."

He staggers around us and heads down the path.

"You okay?" Liam asks, looking me up and down.

I shake my head. I feel too numb to cry. "Help me find my phone? He threw it in the woods."

Liam dials my number and turns on his phone's flashlight. The whistling ringtone "Don't Worry, Be Happy" echoes through the trees.

"Same ringtone, huh?" Liam says. I used to drive the hiking group nuts singing that song at the top of my lungs on the trails, ironically to scare off bears. I downloaded that ringtone for Liam's number.

We step over logs and branches and soon find my phone. The screen is cracked, but at least it still works. We walk back out to the clearing.

"I've got to find Grace. I really need to get out of here."

"You shouldn't go back to the fire. Mason might lose his shit. Text Grace and I'll stay with you until she comes."

"Thanks." I send Grace my SOS text.

We make our way down another path to the road. We arrive to where Rusty is parked.

"Can we talk?" I ask. I unlock the doors, and we get in the car.

"I get it why you don't want to be with me anymore, but can we at least be friends?"

He shakes his head and looks away from me. "You don't get it, do you?"

"Get what?"

"Why I can't be around you. Why I can't talk to you. Why I can't even look at you."

"I thought it was because you just wanted to move on."

"Move on?" He looks at me. "How can we move on? Tell me that, Abby. I mean, with everything that's happened, have you actually been able to just move on?"

"I meant you moving on from me. From us."

He looks away, clenches his jaw. "Don't you see? There's no moving on. Every night, I wake up in a cold sweat. I hear you screaming. That horrible, terrified scream. Every single night." Tears well in his eyes. "And every time I see you, every time, I'm reminded of what a fucking coward I am." Tears run down his face. He wipes them off with his sleeve.

I'm in total shock. "What are you talking about?"

"I saw it. The whole thing. When the grizzly had you in its mouth. Flopping you around. What did I do? I ran. Some boyfriend, eh? I ran away as fast as I could, like a fucking weakling."

"But the bear went after you, too."

"Yeah, but I hardly got a scratch, and the bear went back to you for another round. I left you and did nothing to help. How's that for courage? How's that for integrity?" Liam shakes his head. "How's that for love?" Now he's sobbing. Tears and snot run down his face. "I was only thinking of saving myself." He covers his face with his hand. I put my hand on his arm.

"It was a perfectly natural reaction to run away from danger," I say. "I probably would have done the same thing. What happened to me is not your fault, Liam. Shit happens, you know that. You can't blame yourself."

"You could have died, Abby."

"But I didn't die."

"Well, I wish I did." His body shakes with each sob. Grace walks toward the car. Liam opens the door and gets out. He wipes his face one more time and disappears through the trees.

***

"With Mason at the party, I should never have left you alone," Grace says as I drive her home.

"It wasn't your fault, Grace."

"If Liam hadn't come along, who knows what could have happened." She looks really worried.

"As I've told you, I can handle it."

"And speaking of Liam. Ho-ly shit," Grace says. "He's been keeping everything bottled up this whole time. It's been bubbling and simmering for almost a year and then like a volcano, he exploded all over you."

"It sure explains a few things. I don't know how to feel right now. Relieved? Worried? Angry? Guilty?"

"Don't you start feeling guilty just because Liam does. He's going to have to figure it out himself. But if he carries it around for too much longer, he's going to crack up."

Grace is not only sweet but a pretty wise soul.

By the time I turn down my driveway, I feel physically shaken and emotionally beaten up. Mason and Liam mega-trauma in one night. *Way* too much to deal with, and I'm exhausted. When I drive up to the house, I see Dad through the window. I wish he'd already gone to bed. After I park, I breathe deeply several times and try to hold it together.

In the living room, Dad's sorting through all his hiking gear that's strewn on chairs, the floor, and the couch.

"What's going on?" I ask.

"Hiking Ribbon Creek tomorrow."

"You? Hiking?"

"Don't sound so surprised."

"Who are you going with?"

Dad smiles as he rubs a wax sealant into his hiking boots. "A woman I met downtown for a drink."

"You had another date and didn't tell me?"

"Can't a man keep anything to himself around here?"

"Nope. I have to report back to Jeannie and Gramz. I'm the eyes and ears on your dating life."

Dad shakes his head. "Okay, in a nutshell, I like her."

"What's her name?"

"Angela."

"And..."

"And she's thirty-nine, divorced, no kids, and she's the executive director of a nonprofit organization that promotes environmental concerns." Dad pulls the old, worn laces out of his hiking boots.

"Does she look the same as her profile pic?"

"No."

"What? Not her, too!"

"She looks even better in person." He smiles again as he unwraps a package of new laces and weaves them through his boot.

"That's promising." I pick up his daypack and sniff it. "Pretty musty-smelling."

"Hasn't been out of the basement in years."

"Well, it's about time you air it out," I say and then pick up a camping knife. "And this sure is rusty."

Dad looks up. "I hope *I'm* not too rusty on the trail. Can't remember the last time I did a strenuous hike in the mountains."

"Let's hope Angela the environmentalist goes easy on you."

Dad nods.

I pick up the hiking map from the table. It has Mom's writing on it—GPS coordinates. Right beside the map is a can of bear spray. It might be the same can that I couldn't get to fast enough.

"How was your party?" Dad asks.

"Same old, same old. For some reason I thought things, people, would be different a year later. But not much has changed." Obviously that's not entirely true. No way can I tell him about Mason, or he'd surely call the police. Besides, I handled it. At least I think I did. And I don't want to tell Dad about Liam—at least not right now. He wasn't at all impressed with how Liam suddenly cut off all communication with me at a time when I really needed him.

"And yet so much has changed for you," Dad says.

He doesn't know the half of it.

"Yeah, it sure has."

"Oh, a letter came for you today from Dr. Van der Meer's office. I put it in your room on your dresser."

"Thanks. I'm heading to bed. Have fun on the hike, and, by the way, I'll be wanting a full report tomorrow night."

"Roger that. Nite, kiddo." Dad whistles as he picks up his other hiking boot and brand-new lace.

Haven't heard him whistle since before Mom's death.

I flop onto my bed and hold my arm, still sore where Mason clamped his firm grip. I shake my head, trying to chase away any thoughts of what could have happened. Instead, I replay the scenes from the night all wonky and out of order: Liam getting in my car, Mason's face right in mine, me trying to wrench my phone from Mason's grasp, tears pouring down Liam's face, Mason telling me I slutted around behind his back, Liam calling himself a coward for running away from the bear, me kicking Mason's crotch with all my might, Liam convulsing in sobs, Mason telling me he'd need a bag over my face to have sex with me.

I sit up and open the letter on my dresser. My next surgery is scheduled for eight a.m. on July 17 at the Foothills Hospital. I stuff the letter back into the envelope. I look in the mirror, run my fingers over the dents and bumps on my face that remind me of a topographical map. I try to imagine what I might look like with a cheekbone, and maybe more grafted skin over all the scars. Will I be transformed into a different person? Someone who likes and accepts herself a whole lot more?

TRUST

In my dream I'm alone, hiking through a forest, looking up at the massive pine trees, breathing in the smell of fresh air and damp soil, listening to the birds. I see her up ahead, pawing at the ground, searching for bugs and ants to eat. Her cubs are wrestling with each other close by. She looks up and sees me. Doesn't move. Just stares. Instead of feeling terrified like I usually do, I feel a strange sense of peace as I slowly walk toward her.

I open one eye and look at my clock. Seven fifty-three. In the morning! Saturday morning! I shut my eyes again and think about my dream. After the night I had, why was my dream so serene? I'm usually terrified in my bear dreams—running, scrambling up the tree, tearing skin on my hands and legs, flying out of the tree, my body being dragged in the bear's mouth.

I pick up the bear carving from my bedside table. The smooth wood feels soothing in my hand. For some reason, it looks different today, joyful even.

***

I drive west along the Elbow River Valley, right in the foothills, with the Rocky Mountains in clear view. Only sun and blue sky ahead. I have a tightness in my chest, obviously my chickenshit association with mountains is still alive and well. Not sure why today is the day, but I feel ready to face my fear. My mind teleports me into the mountains. Hiking. Rock climbing. Backpacking. Excitement. Fun. Love. Liam. Bear. Fear. Anxiety. Sadness. Loss. Liam.

Before I left the house, of course I checked the bear report, and, as of this morning, no bears have been sighted anywhere near this area. Although it's not a guarantee, it's some comfort at least. I avoid the provincial park campsite with its wall-to-wall RVs, dirt bikes, boom boxes, and too many screaming kids. Instead, I drive slowly down a remote, bumpy road—praying I don't bottom-out Rusty—to an out-of-the-way picnic area that Liam and I had discovered. We mostly came here as a private place to make out.

I park my car at the very end of the road, look west toward the craggy mountains, and check in on my heart. Calm, steady beats. No light-headedness, no sweating, and the tightness in my chest is gone. What do you know? A first in almost a year. I walk down the overgrown path through the trees to the creek. Kick off my sandals, roll up my jeans, and wade into the stream. I remember family camping trips when Jeannie and I were little and used to play in ice-cold mountain streams. Always in the mountains.

I sit down on a patch of grass by the river and take everything in. The splotches of snow on the peaks in the distance, shrunken by the spring warmth. The giant trees lining the river. The river whooshing and gurgling over the rocks. I have an urge to hike up the ridge close by. Something has changed in me. There's no way I could have done this a few months ago.

I look at the view around me and breathe in the mountain air.

***

When I drive up to the house, Dad is on the back porch untying his mud-covered hiking boots. So much for new laces.

"Doesn't look like you have any injuries. Angela the environmentalist obviously went easy on you," I say, walking toward the house.

"I did pretty well for an old guy who hasn't hiked in a few years."

"So?"

"So what?" Dad scrapes off clumps of mud from his boots.

"How was it?" I ask.

"You know how beautiful Ribbon Creek is."

"Not the hike. How were things with Angela?"

"Fine."

"Dad, *fine* is just not going to cut it when I have to report out."

"We had a lovely day together."

"And…"

"And, we're going out for dinner tomorrow night."

"Sounds promising. You must really like her."

"It's early days, but we do share a lot of interests and values."

"And you think she's attractive."

"Yes, I think she's attractive. I hope that's enough to report out because that's all you're getting." He starts unpacking his gear. Dad's doing what he said we both should do—move forward as best we can.

I go up to my room, lie on my bed, and turn on my laptop. I check out the University of Calgary undergraduate programs. A screen comes up: *Pursue Your Passion*. I type in *Education* and check the admission requirements. An average of seventy-five percent. Check—I got eighty-five percent. Three approved courses. Check—math, English, bio (fingers crossed). Optional courses. Check—drama and phys ed. I carefully read through all the information about a concurrent degree in Education and Drama. Is teaching drama my life's purpose? How will I know?

***

Simon and I eat pistachio caramel-swirl ice cream while finishing an Italian movie called *The Invisible Boy* about a thirteen-year-old boy who is shy, unpopular at school, and in love with a girl named Stella. After he puts on a costume for a Halloween party, he becomes invisible. If only it were that easy.

Simon finishes his last spoonful from his third helping and puts his bowl on the coffee table.

"Pretty decent movie, eh?" I say.

"It was okay." He clicks off the TV.

"What's up with you? You're being weird tonight."

He rests his forearms on his knees, looks down at the floor. His bushy brown hair covers his face. He sighs. "Would you hate me if I—"

"If you what?"

"If I asked Olivia to grad?" He says the words quickly then cringes, waiting for me to blow up.

"What the hell? You know Liam bailed on me."

"It's just that she's new here and had to move right at the end of high school, which really sucks because—"

"You mean you're going to ditch me for the new girl just because she shares your love of computer languages like Mouse, Squirrel, Unicorn—"

"Uni*con*, not Unicorn."

"Olivia doesn't know you worth shit compared to me. It's graduation, Simon. This is an important milestone for us."

"It's just that—"

"That what?"

"I like her, okay?"

I try to quickly translate Simon-speak in my head. "You mean you *like her* like her?"

"Yeah, I think so." Simon's cheeks flush.

"Do you bounce between exhilaration, racing heart, euphoria, loss of appetite, and anxiety, panic, and fear?" I ask.

"What?"

"Do you think about her all the time? Does every song you hear remind you of her? Do you finish each other's sentences?"

"You're nuts."

We're quiet for a long time.

"But do you like her in the sexy-dreams sense of liking her?"

Simon sighs heavily. "I think so. Maybe. I don't really know."

I try to unravel my jumble of emotions. For me: anger, betrayal, generally just pissed right off. For Simon: relief, anticipation, happiness, hope.

"Maybe she wouldn't mind if you came with us." Simon's voice is quiet and contrite. "She knows you're my best friend."

"I'd rather go alone, or not go at all, than be your third wheel."

"Do you hate me?" Simon asks.

"Yeah, I do." But I don't sound very convincing.

UNFRAMED

I have bio, first class of the day. And my first glimpse of Liam since the bush party. Although Serena sits close beside him, he seems to be leaning away from her. This could just be my brain playing tricks on me.

An image of a human digestive tract is projected on the screen at the front. The bulgy curved stomach sits on top of the large and small intestines, which look like one long, folded-up sausage.

"The appendix is considered a vestigial organ. Can anyone guess what that means?" Mr. Jessop asks.

"It means that scientists haven't a clue what its function is," Paul says.

"Almost, but not quite," says Jessop. "A vestigial structure or organ is one that's lost all or most of its original function, or has evolved into a new function. Any other examples of a vestigial structure? Serena?"

"Wisdom teeth?" she says.

"Yes, and I'm sure some of you have already had them extracted. Another example. Abby?"

Liam turns around and looks right at me. "Male nipples?" I say, and the class laughs. Liam keeps looking at me and smiles. I smile back, remembering Liam's nipples, with little tufts of hair sprouting up around them. It looked kind of funny considering he doesn't have any hair on his chest.

"Interesting example. They are vestigial in a different way. They're not left over from an evolutionary event, but instead from an embryological or developmental one. All foetuses effectively begin life in the womb as females. But when a Y chromosome is present, the foetus will produce hormones like testosterone and develop into a male. This makes nipples on males pretty much just decorative."

"Oh yeah," says Paul, rubbing his chest around his nipples.

***

After class, I pack my books into my backpack. Serena is chattering away at Liam, who is lingering at the door, watching me, obviously waiting for me. My heart's getting another workout—I feel both excited and anxious. When Serena notices his eyes are on me, she leaves looking pissed off. Liam follows me out of the classroom and we walk down the hall.

"What about the arrector pili?" Liam says, pointing to the goose bumps that seem to permanently cover my bone-rack body.

"The what?"

"The arrector pili are tiny muscles that cause the hairs on your body to stand up when you get cold."

"So?"

"So, if you're a furry woodland creature, this would provide insulation, but people aren't hairy enough for there to be any effect. Therefore, the muscles are vestigial."

"Still reading *Science* magazine, I see."

Liam's quiet for a bit. "Sorry I went apeshit on you the other night," he says.

"At least I finally know what's going on with you."

"I've given myself the I'm-such-an-effing-coward talk in the mirror about a million times," Liam says. "I didn't think I'd ever have the balls to say it to you." We come to a T-intersection in the hallway and stop. "I've been such an asshole to you, haven't I?"

"Yep."

"I'm sorry about that. About everything. See you around, Abby."

"Yep." I feel incredibly deflated as I watch him walk down the hall. I was hoping for way more from him.

I push open the door to the washroom to find Serena sitting on the floor, legs splayed out. She looks dazed as two grade nines awkwardly step over her to wash their hands in the sink.

"Serena?" I say.

She looks up at me. "Were you talking to Liam?"

I nod.

"Were you talking about me?'

"No, of course not. Are you okay?" She shakes her head. I sit down on the floor beside her.

"I've got to get out of here or I'll go batshit crazy," she says.

"Yeah, school can do that to a person."

"Not just school. I've got to leave home. Get as far away from this place as I can. If I don't I...I..."

"What's going on?" I ask.

"My parents don't know me. They don't even *want* to know me. They barely care about my marks, don't want to hear about what I think or how I feel. Ever. I hear all the time how pretty I am, but that's the only part of me they see. The only part they know. Just the surface. And even after all the face creams and makeup and designer jeans and organic food my mother buys for me, I'll never be good enough, pretty enough, for her." Serena looks at me, tears welling in her eyes. "Get this—she even signed me up for Weight Watchers. A precautionary measure, she told me."

"That's just sick," I say.

"Not according to *Mommy*," Serena says. "And it's getting harder and harder not to believe her." I put my arm around her shoulders.

I can't help but wonder that if self-acceptance is this difficult for a girl like Serena, how are the rest of us supposed to pull it off?

"Are you going to be okay?" I ask.

"Yeah, I guess," Serena says. But I'm worried about her.

I'm late for drama, so I hurry down the hallway to the stairs. Schultzy walks toward me with an uncharacteristically stern look on her face. "I need you to come to my office."

"Why? Something wrong?" I ask.

"I guess we'll find out soon enough. I've left a few messages for your father, but he hasn't called back."

"Schultzy, you're scaring me. What's going on?" I follow her into her office where Mason, Dax, Mr. Hardy, and a woman police officer are all standing around. Schultzy closes the door. Mason smirks and Dax gives me the dirtiest look ever. This can't be good.

"Abby, this is Constable Kozma," Mr. Hardy says. The cop nods in my direction. "It's come to our attention that you're selling drugs to students in this school."

"You've got to be kidding me," I say. "I don't do drugs, I don't even smoke pot."

"She's totally lying," Mason says.

I pull my phone out of my purse and find the photos I took of Mason and Dax at the bush party with the pot.

"See?" I hand my phone to the cop. "I'm not the one here who does drugs."

She doesn't look overly impressed with my evidence. Hands my phone back.

"Abby's the one who gave us the pot. She's one of the main dealers at Rocky View High," Dax says.

"I've been away from school for months, and I bet that hasn't stopped either of you from getting high every single day," I say.

The police officer hands me a piece of paper. "Five other students signed a statement saying that you sold them drugs. Even prescription painkillers." Everyone on the list is from Mason's posse.

"This is total bullshit." I slam the paper on the desk. "These are all Mason and Dax's friends. They'd jump off a cliff if they were told to."

"Who else would have easy access to OxyContin in this school?" Mason asks.

"Come on Schultzy, you don't believe this, do you?" I ask.

"This is a serious allegation that we have to investigate," she says quietly.

"Well, if you really need something to investigate, Mason and Dax have been bullying me since the day I came back to school. Sending me horrible messages on Facebook, calling me names, physically intimidating me."

"You're lying," Mason says.

"And let's not forget *Bear Bait*," I say.

"Come on, how can you blame us for that?" Dax says. "Where's your proof?"

Mason belts out a snigger. "She's just blaming us because she finally got caught."

"He's the one lying," I say.

"Let's deal with one issue at a time," Mr. Hardy says.

"I need to search your locker," Constable Kozma says to me.

"Schultzy, you know me. You know I don't do drugs and would never sell them."

She gives me a sympathetic look. My heart sinks thinking about my locker that, of course, isn't locked. Too easy for Mason and Dax to plant some drugs. A slideshow plays through my mind: Dad and me in Hardy's office; Hardy handing me a letter with *Expelled* stamped across in bold red letters; me cleaning out my locker; the whole teaching staff and student body lined up on either side of the long hallway watching me leave in disgrace; passing Mr. Owen in the line, shaking his head; exiting a paddy wagon, handcuffed; into the police station; mug shots—front and side; Dad, Jeannie, and Grandma visiting me in prison, where I'm wearing a bright orange jumpsuit.

Mason and Dax smirk at each other and at me with their arms crossed like tough guys, as I open my locker door and stand back. I feel dizzy as the cop rifles through my stuff, handing Schultzy my books, notebooks, pencil case. She checks all the pockets in my hoodie. Picks up my bear figurine and inspects it closely. I hold out my hand and she gives it to me. I put it in my pocket, rub the smooth surface to help calm my nerves.

The locker has been emptied. "There are no drugs in this locker," Constable Kozma says and starts putting everything back in. A shiver of relief starts at the top of my head and goes to the bottom of my feet.

Mason and Dax look totally shocked. "What?! There has to be," Mason says. "I saw a bag of pot in there this morning. Maybe she already sold it to somebody."

Mr. Hardy looks sceptical.

The cop gestures to the girls' washroom. "Mrs. Schultz, would you mind joining us?"

Schultzy nods and takes my arm as we follow the cop into the washroom. When we walk in, a few girls are fixing their makeup and brushing their hair. They look shocked to see the cop and quickly pack up and leave.

With my arms outstretched, Constable Kozma pats me down. I'm only wearing a T-shirt and jeans, not many places to hide a bag of pot, or even a bag of pills for that matter. As Schultzy looks on, the cop pats down my back and legs. A grade ten girl opens the bathroom door, sees me being searched, and quickly leaves.

"Nothing," the cop says to Schultzy, then she turns to me. "This investigation isn't over yet, Abby. A serious allegation has been made against you, and I'll be interviewing the students who signed the statement."

We leave the washroom, and Kozma shakes her head at Hardy.

"This puts the issue to rest," Hardy says. "For now, anyway." Even though I know I'm innocent, his severe look makes me feel shaky.

"Letting her off is total bullshit," Dax says.

"Back to class. All of you," Hardy says. Kozma follows him to his office.

Mason faces me and mouths *ugly bitch* so that Schultzy can't see. He traces a finger down his face exactly where the scars are on my forehead and cheek. I flip him the bird while pretending to scratch my forehead. I turn and walk away, feeling strangely empowered.

Schultzy walks me down the hallway. "I told you on your first day back at school to come and see me if anyone was giving you problems."

"And I'm sure you know that snitching on bullies almost always makes everything worse. Besides, I'm handling it."

"Handling it? Looks like it's escalated to me," Schultzy says.

She doesn't know the half of it.

"Do you have any proof that it was Dax and Mason who were the cyberbullies?" she asks. "Any emails? Facebook messages?"

I shake my head. "Like it said on a website I found, block whoever is bullying you online. So I did."

"Good advice. But promise me from here on in that if there is even a hint of bullying from either Dax or Mason, you'll come to me right away. Everyone in school has the right to be treated with dignity and respect. No one deserves to be bullied."

Knowing full well I probably won't tell Schultzy a thing, I nod. She heads to her office.

People look at me funny as I make my way down the hallway, and I don't think it's my scarred face for a change. It's obvious that news of me being the Rocky View High drug lord has probably been texted, tweeted, and shared around the whole school. I stop at my locker—unlocked, of course. Note to self: bring your lock to school. I dump my books in my locker and head for lunch.

Dad texts.

Mr. Hardy just called, told me what happened.

Ya, totally insane

Anything you need to share with me?

For real? Is he so disengaged that he thinks I could actually be a drug dealer?!

Of course not!!!!!!!

Okay, just checking. You can tell me all about this fiasco tonight.

Oh joy.

With big grins, Simon and Jackson almost skip down the hall toward me.

"Why so excited? Finally figured out how to hack the Pentagon?" I ask.

"Something almost as good," Jackson says.

"Come on, follow us," Simon says, walking quickly toward the door. Across the parking lot, I see Hardy walk Constable Kozma to her cruiser. My whole body shivers. I could still be in deep shit.

Simon and I hop in the front seat of his Jeep, Jackson in the back. Simon unlocks the glove box. "Look inside," he says.

A musty marijuana smell immediately wafts out. "What the hell?" I ask, looking around to make sure no one is ready to take photos with their cell phones.

"Jackson and I were walking down the hall and saw Dax and Mason hanging out by your locker. I thought maybe they were going to write something else on it."

"So we hid around the corner and watched," Jackson says.

"Mason opened your *unlocked* locker and put something inside. We waited until they left and then opened your locker and found that bag of pot."

"They were obviously going to try to frame you for possession or something, so we locked it in here," Jackson says, sounding rather proud of himself.

"Holy shit. You guys totally saved my ass. I got hauled into Schultzy's office with Hardy and a cop. All of Mason and Dax's fellow goons signed a paper that I was selling drugs at the school. I even got body-searched."

Simon and Jackson high-five each other.

"So, what are we going to do with it?" I say.

"Give it back to its rightful owner?" Simon says, starting to put it his backpack.

"Wait." I dig in my purse for a piece of paper and a pen, and write a note. *Dear Mason, I think you may have misplaced this. Enjoy killing the few remaining brain cells you were born with.* Decide not to sign it. I open the ziplock and stuff the note inside. I think better of it and take the note out, scrunch it up and put it in my pocket.

I shouldn't really be anywhere near a bag of pot at this moment, but I follow Simon and Jackson to Mason's truck, keeping an eye out for any spectators.

"Well, isn't that convenient?" Simon says, pointing to a rather large hole in the passenger window of the truck, cracks snaking out all around the jagged edges. Simon tries to stuff the bag through the hole, which, of course, makes the plastic bag rip. Most of the pot spills out on the seat.

"Should we tell Hardy to search Mason's truck for the pot?" Jackson asks.

"Are you out of your mind?" I say. "I want this over with. I need a truce with these assholes."

But as we head back to the school, I know this is far from over.

CLIMBING THE WALLS

We're barreling east down Highway 1, leaving the rolling hills and smell of fresh cow manure behind us. Grace drives Briar and me in her mom's Volvo to the climbing wall at Eagle Glen Community Center in northwest Calgary. Normally, I would be ecstatic to spend a few hours of my school day climbing, even if it is just a little wall in a gym. But I'm so out of shape and my leg with the torn muscle and tendon doesn't work like it used to. I'm so anxious that I've totally lost my climbing mojo.

"I've got serious vertigo, absolutely *hated* the climbing wall last year, and the year before, and I'm sure I'll hate it again this year," Briar says. "Why do they keep making us come here?"

"Because it's actually a blast," Grace says.

Briar braids her long hair. "Yeah, but you two are mutant mountain goats. My knees start shaking when I'm about a foot off the ground."

"Abby's the mutant. I'm a hiker, not a climber," Grace says. "The only climbing I've done is on this wall in phys ed last year."

"I'm the mutant, all right," I say quietly as I look out the window. I feel jittery at the thought of gearing up.

"Wish I'd come up with the menstrual-cramps excuse before Serena did," Briar says, pouting. "And why does this have to be a mixed class? I don't want to make an ass out of myself in front of the guys."

"How about a little whine with your cheese?" Grace says. She and I share a smile.

We pull into the parking lot just as Liam gets out of his mom's car, along with Jemal, Justin, and Gus. The thought of climbing sends my brain cells right back to the mountains. Clinging to a rock wall with Liam right beside me. Totally blissed out.

"Always thought the climbing wall looked like a huge chunk of gray rock covered with weird-shaped, colorful pimples," Briar says as we walk into the climbing-wall gym.

I look up at the wall, about eighty feet tall. A shrimp compared to climbs I've done in the Rockies. Although climbing an actual rock face is way more fun, grabbing on to those colorful pimples is still good practice.

I see Matt, my old climbing instructor, talking animatedly to Liam. They're probably reminiscing about one of the climbs we all did together. When Matt sees us, he comes up to me.

"Hey!" he says. With his bulging rock-climber biceps, he picks me up right off the ground and spins me around. Liam looks over, amused.

"Matty!"

"Geez, you're as light as a feather. Where's the beef, girl?" he says.

"I'm trying to make myself as unappetizing as possible." Matt hasn't seen me in well over a year, and I'm surprised that he doesn't study my face in the usual strange kind of way that people do post-bear attack.

"Shit, Abby, it's so good to see you. Sorry I've been such a slacker about keeping in touch and all."

"Not to worry, I haven't exactly been venturing far from home. Definitely not into the mountains, if you know what I mean," I say.

"Gotcha. But we miss you out in them there mountains. Coming back soon?"

"Not sure, but I hope to."

"One day at a time, as they say. Let me know when you're ready, and we'll plan an awesome day. Maybe we'll even invite Liam." Matt says "Liam" in a joking way, probably thinks we're still together. Mr. Harris and Ms. Wong gesture to Matt. "Better get this party started," he says and goes to talk to the teachers.

"Abby, who's that hot guy you've been keeping from us?" Briar asks.

"My climbing instructor who quickly became a friend," I say.

"I think it's time for me to take some climbing lessons," says Grace, checking out Matt and his big biceps.

The whole group gathers around Matt in front of the climbing wall. "As I'm sure many of you know, climbing is not only a physical challenge, but also a mental puzzle you're trying to put together as you work your way up the wall, or mountain," he says.

"You have to introduce me to this guy," Grace whispers to me as Matt talks. "I just want to run my hands all over his chiseled body. Gawd, those rippling muscles!"

"As gorgeous and fabulous as you are, he's twenty-one and has a girlfriend who is a national-level sports climber. Matt's totally gaga over Lisa."

"Damn," Grace harrumphs.

Mason, with his red eyes and goofy grin, finally wanders into the gym. Climbing stoned: *so* not a good idea.

"Just to review," Matt says, "since I'm sure you all heard about this last year, there are three golden rules of climbing, and I'm going to ask my star student to demonstrate for you. Abby, would you mind?"

I freeze. I haven't climbed in over a year. What if my leg gives out? What if I can't concentrate?

"Abby?" Matt says.

I lean close to Matt and quietly say, "I can't. I'm way too out of shape. Please ask someone else."

"You've got to get back in the gear sometime, Abby," he says.

I look at Ms.Wong for permission. She nods.

Mason cheers and claps loudly like an idiot. "Way to go, Abby." Don't Harris and Wong see that Mason is seriously stoned?

I slip on my climbing shoes. Pray really hard that I don't make a total fool of myself.

"What's the first rule? Anyone?" Blank stares. "How about Liam, my mediocre student?" Matt jokes.

"Hey now," Liam says with a big smile. "You need straight arms."

"Correct. Abby, can you show us?"

I start up the wall a short ways. I reach to a high grip with my arm extended.

"See how relaxed Abby looks? The weight is on her shoulders and fingers." If Matt only knew how every one of my muscles is as tense as a guitar string. "She's got it goin' on," Matt continues. "That's what we're looking for. Back down, Abby. I swear this girl is part chimpanzee."

Mason makes chimp noises and scratches his belly. He gets a few laughs.

I find my grips and footing back down. I feel awkward and a bit clumsy, like I've never done this before.

"Second golden rule, anyone?" Matt says.

"Find your center of gravity," Justin says.

"Excellent," Matt says. "When climbing, it's important to understand where your center of gravity is and how to make it work for you. It's roughly the middle point of your body. The weight of your body acts from this point. Where you put your center of gravity can decide whether your weight is on your arms or legs. Abby, demonstrate please."

Again, I make my way up the wall. I reach with my right hand, swivel my right hip toward the wall. I reach higher with my left hand, lose my grip, and fall to the ground. Land hard on my butt. Luckily, I wasn't too high.

"Nice recovery," Matt says and helps me up.

"I didn't recover, I fell," I say to Matt. "Maybe someone else should—" But Matt's not having it.

"Up you go again," Matt says to me.

I look up the wall. A year ago, Liam and I would have raced to the top, no problem. I feel quivery as I start again. Grip, swivel my hip toward the wall, grip again.

"See how her butt was tucked in?" Matt says. "If it was sticking out, gravity would naturally pull her away from the wall."

Again, Mason bursts out, "Nice butt action, Abby." Matt is obviously getting annoyed.

"So, if she lets go, the force would rip her off the wall," Matt says. "See how she rotates her hips in, which pulls the center of gravity in toward the wall."

Back down I go. My brain wants to keep going, but my body is fighting it every step of the way.

"Third rule. Can anyone else guess? I'm sure you learned this last year."

"Something about how to use your feet properly?" Grace says, sucking up to the climbing instructor.

"Yes. Third rule is mind your feet. Abby." He gestures for me to head back up.

I place my feet, reach for a grip, pull my hip toward the wall.

"Abby steps on the toe area of her shoe, not the heel or the center of the foot. This helps her reach higher. Then she rotates her foot and steps on her pinkie toe to help pull her hips in toward the wall."

I do reach higher. My body is starting to remember the exhilaration, the flow. I'd forgotten how much I love this. I get lost in my movements, the rhythm, and climb right to the top of the wall. Maybe I will be able to climb mountains again.

Matt calls out to me. "That's my girl."

I look down at Liam's smiling face. He starts clapping and everyone joins in. Mason whistles loudly. I bow, hanging on with one hand, and make my way back down.

Everyone practices the free climb without gear. No one except Liam makes it to the top. I'm actually worried about Mason, but Matt probably knows what's going on because he calls Mason down when he's too high off the ground. Matt also makes sure he is Mason's spotter, holding up his arms to catch Mason's fall.

After the free climb, Matt asks Liam and me to demonstrate lead climbing. He first shows everyone how our gear works and how to do safety checks.

"Our lead climber, Abby, is the one with the harness on. She'll clip her rope every five feet or so into one of the carabiners. Liam is the belayer. He feeds Abby the rope when she goes up and makes sure that if Abby falls, she doesn't splat right back to the ground. Okay, now Abby and Liam will demonstrate how to effectively belay."

I start climbing the wall, clip my rope, climb higher, clip again.

"Watch how Liam pulls the slack, locks, and slides up," Matt says. "Pull, lock, slide. Pull, lock, slide."

I'm now at the top. Look down. It may be me feeling chuffed, but everyone looks kind of impressed. Even Mason. I might be deluding myself.

"Now watch how Liam works the ropes as he lowers Abby down. See how he keeps his hands nice and close to the belay device, how he controls her speed?" Matt says.

I slowly float toward the ground.

"Now, Abby, push away from the wall. I want to show how the belayer catches the lead climber's fall."

I push off the wall in free fall. Liam does his job because my body springs up, stops the fall.

"See how Liam pulled up on the rope? Okay, time to let her down," I hear Matt say.

Liam slowly lowers me down but keeps me hovering in the air, high enough off the ground so I can't touch down. This is a game we used to play when we were first learning to climb—keeping each other hanging in midair.

"Thanks for saving my life," I say, looking down at him.

"No sweat." Liam smiles and finally lowers me until my feet touch the ground.

"Your phone number still the same?" Matt asks me when the class is over. Grace and Briar wait in the wings. Liam looks over at us before he leaves.

"Yup," I say.

"Have you ever climbed Mount Louis, near Lake Louise?"

"Nope, haven't done that climb," I say.

"It's so awesome. Some of my friends are planning a trip in a couple of weeks. I'll text you details."

"Matt, it's just…I'm not sure if I'm up for a climb yet," I say.

"Trust me. I won't let a bear anywhere near you."

"In that case, yeah, let me know when you're going."

"It's been great to see you, Abby. I would be honored to be the one to lure you back to the mountains." Matt gives me a hug and goes to pack up equipment.

"Oh…my…God. He's the whole package and more." Grace links her arm in mine as we head for the door.

"If Matt and his girlfriend ever break up, I want to be the first to know," Briar says, turning around for another look at Matt.

"The lineup is after me, sistah," Grace says as we walk out of the community center.

***

"Justin, huh?" I say to Grace as we eat lunch at a school picnic table.

"He's not really my type—physically, I mean. Is that a really bitchy thing to say?" Grace asks.

"Probably."

"But he is kind of sweet. He was so nervous when he asked me and looked so surprised that I actually said yes." Grace bites into a sandwich.

"Makes sense that he asked you. He's a good buddy of Liam's, so the four of you will probably go together and have a very lovely time," I say, feeling completely and utterly sorry for myself that I'll be the only one of my friends who won't have a date for grad. I try to think positive, happy, self-accepting thoughts, but it's one of those days when the crappy ones keep stomping them down.

"We probably will go with Serena and Liam," Grace says, "but not sure about the lovely time. Think you'll at least go to the banquet and dance?"

"Not sure. It would feel so weird. Who am I going to dance with? My dad?" I twirl my leftover spaghetti with my fork, but I've lost my appetite. I crunch into a carrot stick instead. I look over and see Simon and Olivia at another table holding hands, talking, laughing. Simon looks so happy, which makes me feel even more alone.

"My mom's coming to the dinner, too, with her new boyfriend, Howie, who is so incredibly annoying you wouldn't believe it."

"How so?" I ask.

"For one thing, he really likes to tell me how often he and my mom 'do it.'"

"Seriously? Yuck!"

"I know! I wish Mom had asked me first before she bought him a ticket," Grace says.

"Gawd, if I do go to grad, I wonder if my dad will want to bring Angela the environmentalist."

"Angela who?"

"A woman he just started dating."

"Your dad is dating? Since when?"

"Since my sister and I signed him up on an online dating site."

"My mom sure could have given him some pointers," Grace says, finishing off her sandwich. "I swear she has been on at least a hundred online dates in the past six months, and I'm not exaggerating. Coffees, lunches, picnics, walks, drinks, dinners."

"Remember in ninth grade when we tried to fix up my dad and your mom?" I say.

"Oh my God! Is that when your dad picked you up at my place and we made him stay and drink chocolate milk until my mom came home from work?"

"Yeah. Total dislike at first sight."

"My mom is *so* not your dad's type—the cleavage queen with her fake nails and eyelashes. Your dad is cool, down to earth." Grace wipes her apple on a napkin. "Abbs, about grad. You're the one who said it's just one day and then it'll be over. Like Christmas." She bites into her shiny red apple.

"True. But what will I miss if I don't go?"

UNREHEARSED

I'm not going to leave this life with any regrets, just memories," Tali says as she reaches the end of her monologue rehearsal in front of the drama class. "I'm going to love, to respect people, to detach myself from all negative energy. I'm going to try everything I want to try—skydiving, snake charming, belly dancing." Tali uses strong, repeated hand gestures to emphasize her points, which comes across as a bit over the top. "I will take risks and allow the unexpected. As Oprah Winfrey said…"

Dax, Mason, and a few other people burst out laughing when Oprah is mentioned, so Tali stops, looks hurt. Pushes her glasses higher on her nose.

"Show some respect, please," Mr. Owen says, looking right at Mason and Dax. Mason crosses his arms, sighs too loudly, looks bored. Dax follows suit and crosses his arms. "Continue Tali."

"As Oprah said, 'The only people who never tumble are those who never mount the high wire. This is your moment.'" Tali pauses and looks at as many people in the eye as possible. "This moment belongs to all of us. Let's make the most of our precious lives." Tali finishes and everyone claps, but not very enthusiastically.

"Comments, questions, feedback for Tali. Anyone?" Owen says.

There's an awkward silence. No one wants to say anything.

Finally, I say, "I think some of the things you have to say are quite compelling. You're challenging everyone to live life to the fullest, which is a good thing."

Tali smiles, looks hopeful.

"Anyone else?" Owen says.

"I agree with Abby," Carter says, "but I think you might want to tone down some of the air punches. It kind of detracts from your message."

"Does that make sense to you, Tali?" Owen asks.

Tali nods.

"Mason, any constructive feedback for Tali?" Owen asks.

Mason lets out another big sigh. "Maybe don't be so earnest. It sounds fake—like you're overacting. Just speak like you're talking to a friend or something. And to be honest, I'm not sure about quoting Oprah."

"Well I think Oprah is an amazing woman who many people admire," Tali says. Mason turns away from both Owen and Tali and pretends to throw up.

"Okay, thanks for your comments everyone," Mr. Owen says. "What I have to say is not just for Tali, but for everyone to keep in mind. Every movement—whether crossing the stage or making a small gesture—should have a real motivation. Don't add gestures or movements for effect, it will only distract your audience. Make sense?"

Tali nods but looks disappointed in the critique.

"Another big round of applause for Tali," Owen says. Tali heads for her chair. "Since we're running out of time, let's quickly move on. Next up is Abby who will rehearse her monologue, 'Dancing with the Bear.'"

What? I didn't know I was up today. Owen hasn't even approved my second draft. I hear "whoa" and "what the...?" and a few "holy shit." Holy shit, indeed. And that reaction is just from my title. What am I doing? My cheeks are burning hot, which means my scars will be even more visible. My scars are my only props. I search through my binder and find a printed-off copy of my monologue with Owen's red scratches throughout.

I walk to the front of the class. Since I haven't memorized my monologue yet, I hold the script in my hand. The paper shakes. I don't remember being this nervous in a rehearsal before. Ever. I look around at everyone. Mason gives me a look that makes me feel like he punched me in the gut.

I clear my throat and begin. "The s-strange thing was I...I didn't feel anything, at least n-not while it was happening..."

I try to keep my head up, make eye contact with the audience, but it's as if my eyes become glued to the pages in my hands. I just keep going and don't stop. Trip on my words. Stutter and stall. Lose my place on the page. When I finish, I look up. A tiny white feather floats in front of my face. I sigh deeply and send the feather flying.

Everyone is quiet. Dead quiet. Even Mr. Owen. I think I hear the feather touch the ground. Everyone just stares at me for what feels like an eternity. I can't read their faces. Except for Mason—he shakes his head as if I'm a total waste of time.

"Well...thank you, Abby," Mr. Owen says, clearing his throat, straining to be diplomatic. "Any comments, questions, feedback for

Abby?" Everyone either looks blankly at me or avoids eye contact altogether.

Saved by the bell.

I stay seated and let everyone file out of the drama room ahead of me. I really want to give Mason and Dax a big head start in hopes they will just leave for the day, rather than stay on the stairs and harass me.

"It's clear to me, and the entire class for that matter, that you haven't been doing much rehearsing on your own," Mr. Owen says and sits on the chair beside me.

"That obvious, huh?"

"You're one of my most talented students, Abby. And I expected more from you. Especially this year, your final grade twelve performance."

Can't he give me a break? I was mauled by a bear and was in hospital for months. Typical take-no-shit Owen.

"Yeah, well, I totally forgot that my rehearsal was today," I say, sounding incredibly lame.

"You should have been preparing well in advance of today's rehearsal, including writing another draft. What you've submitted so far is not up to your standard."

"But I've worked so hard on it. I really have. Wrote everything you asked me to—what's meaningful to me, what I've learned from the experience. I guess I still don't know what you want from me." My voice is loud. I'm suddenly very emotional, trying not to cry.

"Your work reads more like a social studies report than a dramatic monologue. Dig deeper and find the heart of the story, Abby. I know you have it in you."

I feel like crap.

"Are you aware that the Graduate Drama Showcase is the week after next?" Owen asks.

"What?! So soon?" I'm in shock. Really and truly in shock. Where has the time gone?

"Yes, so soon," Mr. Owen strokes his ginger beard. "Your monologue has the potential to be powerful. If you're willing to put in the work, you have a good chance of winning the Theater on the Edge summer internship. Don't blow that opportunity."

"I won't." Owen stands up. "Mr. Owen, are you leaving right now?"

"Yes." He looks at his cell phone. "I'm late for a staff meeting."

I stand and sling my backpack over my shoulder. "I'll go down with you, and you can tell me more about the internship."

Owen and I leave the drama room and head down the stairs.

"From what I know of the workshop," Owen says, "they'll be covering a variety of acting techniques, speech, movement, playwriting, and stagecraft."

As usual, Mason, Dax, and company are waiting for me on the landing.

"Anything else you can tell me?" I ask Owen.

"There will probably be some on-camera work, audition prep, and such," Owen says and nods at Mason and Dax. "And then, of course, a chance to be in their summer festival, which draws hundreds of people each year."

As we walk past, I give Mason and Dax the best fake (crooked) smile I can muster. Mason gives me the finger.

"That sounds amazing," I say and breathe a humungous sigh of relief as we walk down the last flight of stairs.

***

Simon is waiting for me in the parking lot.

"I never see you anymore," I say. "It's as if you've grown an Olivia appendage. Speaking of Olivia…"

"No, we haven't had sex yet, if that was what you were going to ask."

"I wouldn't ask you anything so personal," I say with a huge grin.

"Since when?" The Jeep fob beeps, a loud click unlocks the doors. "And what about you? You seem to be hanging with the Sticky Hive as if you never left," says Simon.

"Oh, I've left all right. I have absolutely nothing in common with Serena and Briar, but at least Grace is coming around." I climb into the passenger seat.

"Yeah, I don't see her shadowing Serena as much these days." Simon puts on his seat belt. "Speaking of Serena, I overheard her and Liam talking at lunch today."

"What about?"

"Apparently Liam got accepted into first year sciences at Queen's University."

"Where's that?"

"Kingston, Ontario."

"Why is everyone moving to Ontario? First you and now Liam!"

"Don't take it personally, Abby." Simon starts the Jeep.

"What else were Liam and Serena talking about?"

"Well, turns out Serena has now decided to apply to Queen's, too," says Simon.

"Figures." I get a sharp pain in my chest, right where my heart is.

"It is fitting, if nothing else. The Queen Bee going to Queen's," says Simon, chuckling to himself as he pulls out of the school parking lot.

***

I wave at Simon as he leaves my house. When I open the back door, Ruby runs to greet me, whines until I scratch behind her ears, then runs outside.

I open the freezer door and pull out a carton of double-fudge-heaven ice cream and grab a large spoon. I plop down in the family room and stuff a huge spoonful in my mouth. All I can think about is Serena and Liam together at Queen's University. Studying together at the library, walking hand in hand across the campus, drinking beer at pub night with all their new friends, sneaking into each other's dorm rooms. I take my phone out of my pocket and press Home.

"Siri, should I apply to Queen's University?"

"I'm sure I don't know," she says.

Me neither, Siri. Me neither.

***

Nadine stands in front of the room for part two of the Facing It teen workshop. "I'm hoping tonight that everyone will learn at least a few strategies to move toward positive self-esteem and self-acceptance."

She writes on the flipchart: Awareness.

"Awareness. Being alert, consciously aware of your thoughts, feelings, words, and actions. Your self-esteem is a reflection of what you think and how you feel about yourself. Therefore, it's important to be aware of thoughts and feelings that undermine your self-esteem. When you start noticing critical, judgmental, and sabotaging self-talk, you're on your way to upgrading the software, or brain pathways, in your mind." Jade gently elbows me and smiles. Just what she talked to me about after the last workshop.

Next, Nadine writes *Choice*. "Choice is the act of picking one alternative over another. Consciously choosing the thoughts and actions that support your positive self-esteem and self-acceptance. Can anyone give me a good example?"

"Instead of always turning down invitations," says the girl who commented on the beauty magazines, "start accepting them and believe that the person asking sincerely wants your company." It makes me think of how I planned on weaseling out of Grace's invitation to the bush party.

"Excellent, Paula. Your example is both choosing a new thought process—maybe this person really does want me around—as well as an action—accepting the invitation and going to the party, or on the date, or whatever."

Nadine continues. "Becoming more self-accepting means you non-judgmentally affirm the person you are, no matter what strengths, weaknesses, flaws, personality disorders, or facial differences you have. And it's *not* future-oriented: 'I'll be okay when…' or 'Maybe I'll accept myself after my next surgery.' Self-acceptance is about already being fine with who you are, right here and now. Even if you don't yet feel it in your bones, keep telling yourself: 'I am confident. I am worthy. I am acceptable just the way I am, flaws and all.' Other statements?" Some people pipe up.

"I'm smart."

"I'm funny."

"I have a different kind of beauty."

"I'm talented," I say with some confidence.

"Well done, everyone," Nadine says. She writes Change on the chart. "Change is where the rubber meets the road. It's where you practice the choices you've made. This doesn't mean there won't be times when you feel like crap—less than, or not enough. But when those feelings come up, be aware, shift to more positive thoughts and feelings. In order to change, you have to keep practicing this over and over again."

"I'm not saying I'm the queen of self-acceptance or anything," Jade tells the group. "But sometimes you just have to fake it until you make it."

This makes me smile. I've got a whole lot of faking ahead of me.

THE GIANT PETTING ZOO

I work for hours tearing apart my monologue and then reconstructing it. I think I finally nailed it—but then again, I thought the other drafts were brilliant too.

"Dancing with the Bear, by Abby Hughes," I say out loud to myself in the bedroom mirror. My tongue feels like a mousetrap is stuck on the end of it, so I do some enunciation exercises that Owen taught me over the past few years, starting with my new favorite.

"Big black bug bit a big black bear and the big black bear bled black blood. Big black bug bit a big black bear and the big black bear bled black blood." I say that over several times and then try some others: "Can I cook a proper cup of coffee in a copper coffeepot? Yoda met a Yeti on the Plains of Serengeti. Jingle jungle jangle joker. Xylophones exist or so existentialists insist." I keep up the exercises until I get bored, which doesn't take very long.

I look at my face closely in the mirror from every angle. Now that everyone at school has gotten used to my facial "difference," I wonder if anyone really cares about my story. Maybe it's old news by now.

Liam probably already told everyone what happened that day. But then maybe not. He'd have had to confess the guilt he feels, which I'm pretty sure he hasn't wanted to.

I start rehearsing. "The strange thing was I didn't feel anything, at least not while it was happening." I use my full voice, clear and direct. Eyes straight ahead to the mirror, not on the script. "Her bear smell was overpowering, like a hundred dead skunks on a pile of rotting leaves. I buried my hand in her thick, oily fur."

I rehearse my monologue about twenty times, until I finally get it right. Or at least as close to right as I can get it for now. I hear Owen's voice in my head: "If you have rehearsed well, it will be in your muscle memory, and you will be able to just relax and perform."

I lie on my bed, open my laptop. Thankfully, I blocked UR SO FN UGLY, and Mason and Dax obviously figured out that there's no use sending more hurtful stuff. I check out Liam's Facebook profile. Although he hasn't posted anything new on Facebook for months, he recently shared a memory from last year: the two of us at the top of the Cascade Amphitheatre, hamming it up with crossed eyes and stuck-out tongues. There are craggy rocks all around, with a snowy peak sticking up behind us. No comment from Liam, just the photo. Grace, Justin, Gus, mountain climber Matt, and a bunch of others "liked" the memory. Surprise, surprise, there isn't a "like" from Serena. All I remember from that day is we had a big fight on the drive home. I can't even remember what the fight was about—something stupid, I'm sure. I froze him out for a few days. What a bitch I was. He finally called me and we made up. I should have been the one to call him.

I miss Liam and ache to talk to him right now, but I'm too chicken to phone or text him. I check to see if he's on Facebook chat, but he's not, so I "like" the photo and write a comment: *One of our many awesome days together hiking in the Rockies.* As soon as I write the words, I want to delete my comment. I don't want Liam to think I'm creeping him, even though I often do. I leave the comment as is. What do I have to lose?

I check to see if there's anyone else online, but only Briar, Keegan, Devin, and no one else I want to "chat" with. Messenger pings. It's to Liam and me from Matt. *Hey you two, Lisa and I and maybe a few other climbers are heading to Mount Louis on Saturday. Come. We'll already be in Banff, but let's meet up at the base around nine. I belay you can fly!*

Just reading Matt's message makes my heart pound hard. The thought of being in the mountains. Bears. Liam. Joy. The mental gymnastics while climbing. Exhilaration. The risks. My bum leg. Yikes! Finding the perfect holds to grip, placing my feet just right, pulling myself higher. The rush. I send both Matt and Liam a message back: *Ya, sure-cu saturday.*

I can't believe I just did that. What am I thinking? Will I even be able to get out of my car? I can always bail. But what if Liam decides to go?

Matt writes back: *Excellent. Glad to see you're getting "boulder."* Ha ha.

I send him back a smiley face, but it really should be the emoji with the crazy, anxious, wide-open eyes and the little straight line for a mouth.

I can't help myself— I send Liam a text.

Did you get Matt's note on Messenger?

I suddenly feel like I'm too pushy and immediately regret texting him. I stare at my phone for what feels like an eternity until he finally responds.

Ya

Think you'll go?

No, gotta work.

Can't get someone else to work for you?

No

A year ago no one could tear Liam away from the mountains. He would always get someone to work for him if there was a hike or a climb.

K, c u

Yup

Am I the reason why he doesn't want to go climbing? Is it because he feels guilty whenever he's around me? Is he going through his own trauma—as freaked out about being in the mountains as I am?

I feel disappointed. Empty. Sad. Sad that Liam's *so* over me. And sad that I'm *so* not over him.

I go to the "Evolve" Facebook page for some inspiration and solace, and there's oodles of it. Quotes, aphorisms, self-help articles. I close my eyes and scroll down and down. When I open my eyes, this is the quote on my screen:

"Look around. This is how it is. Not how it might have been, or should have been, or how you thought it would be. It is how it is."

I read this over a few times, let the words sink in. I scroll through Matt's Instagram photos. Ninety-five percent of them are of climbing. I know that expression on his face. There are a ton of photos of me with that same look. Total awe and amazement getting to the top of a rock face, gazing across a mountain range at the other peaks, knowing that not many people in the world have seen that same exact view.

***

I slept through my alarm, so I drive as fast as Rusty will carry me down the highway toward Banff to meet Matt and his buddies. When I hit Canmore, the snowy peaks against the blue sky with fluffy white clouds look too perfect somehow. Surreal, like a photoshopped postcard. I realize I'm now right in the mountains. I check myself. No sweating, pounding heart, or shaking. Progress.

When I enter Banff National Park, traffic slows to a crawl, and there's a long line of cars and RVs pulled over to the side of the highway. This pretty much always means there's wildlife close by. Some tourists think the national park plans it—puts the mountain sheep and mountain goats on display just for them, like a petting zoo. Morons!

Although I'm late, I'm also starving, desperate to stop and get the granola bar in my pack, which happens to be in the backseat, out of reach. So when a truck parked on the shoulder pulls out, I take its spot. Sure enough, right beside my car is a young black bear munching on some roots. Perfect. Just perfect. I'm too close. Even though I'm in my car. Protected. I'm *way* too close. Here I go—heart beats wildly, hands get all sweaty, head goes a little dizzy. *I am courageous. I am strong. I am confident. I am courageous. I am strong...*I look out my window at people who are insanely close to the bear, taking pictures. One tourist, very tanned, buff, and handsome enough to be a movie star, starts feeding the bear rice cakes. A wave of rage comes over me, opens my car door, and pushes me outside. My car is the only thing between the bear and me.

"Hey!" I call out to movie-star guy.

He looks over at me, checks out my face, and frowns.

"Yeah, I mean you," I say. Who is this person speaking words out of my mouth? The bear's sharp teeth are on one end of the rice cake, this idiot's hand is on the other. "Are you crazy, or what?"

"Just communing with nature," he says.

"Stop it! Stop right now!" I yell like a crazy person. "That bear is a wild animal. Not only could you get mauled, but you're putting the bear's life at risk."

"Screw off," he says and pulls another rice cake out of his bag.

"You're making the bear feel comfortable near the highway, which means it could get hit by a car." I notice some of the people slowly backing away or heading to their vehicles. I'm on a roll and I can't stop. "And do you know what happens when bears get a taste for people food? They wander into campgrounds and towns like Banff and have conflicts with humans and then guess who pays for it? Usually not the humans. The bear is the one who gets killed. Loses its life because people are careless and stupid. People like you." Tears are pouring down my cheeks.

The jerk turns his back and takes a selfie with the bear behind him. Gives me a dirty look before he heads back to his monster motor home.

I get back in my car and wipe my wet face with my sleeve. The bear looks so calm and peaceful munching on the rice cake, almost looks like its hamming for all the people taking pictures. So trusting that it won't get hit by a car or shot by a wildlife officer. The bear turns and looks right at me. We lock eyes for a long time. It starts chewing again and then wanders off into the forest.

I get a text from Matt.

Where are you? We're all geared up and ready to go.

Sorry, crazy traffic on the highway

I'll stay back and wait for you.

No don't, I'll catch you guys next climb

You sure?

Yup

Remember, Abby-climbing is the only cure for gravity.

A true Matt-ism

Later.

I scroll through the contacts on my phone. "Hey, it's me. What are you up to today?"

***

"He just stared at me for so long," I say as Gramz and I walk along a trail just outside of Banff. Tall trees line the path and there's a reflection of the mountains in the small stream beside us. "It was like he was thanking me or something."

"It took a lot of courage to do what you did, Abby," she says. "Not only standing up to that man, but standing up *for* the bear."

"Don't be too impressed, it was just a black bear." I catch myself. Positive thoughts about myself. I am courageous. I am strong. I am worthy. "No, you're right, Gramz. It was courageous of me, considering what a chicken I've been just being in the mountains, let alone a few feet away from a bear."

"Sounds to me like you're starting to finally make peace with the mother grizzly."

"Not sure about the grizzly, but look at me. I'm walking with you on a mountain trail. Yes, there are busloads of tourists and mountain bikers around us scaring away all living things, including the birds, but I haven't had a meltdown. Not yet, anyway."

"You're doing spectacularly well, sweetie." Gramz smiles and links her arm through mine. I breathe in the earthy forest, one of my favorite smells. I've missed it so much.

"Gramz, do you think I'd make a good drama teacher?"

"I think you'd make an excellent drama teacher. You're a talented actor, you're bright and hardworking, you're a good communicator, and you care about people."

"But how do I know if it's my life's purpose?"

"What excites you? What are you passionate about? What do other people say you're good at? Answer these questions and I'll bet you'll be well on your way to figuring it out."

I am definitely passionate about drama. And when Carter and I taught that improv class, I felt a jolt of energy run through my body. I really connected with the students.

"I still can't believe that high school is going to be over so soon," I say.

"Graduation will be here before you know it. By the way, when we get back, I want to show you something," she says as we head down the path toward town.

***

"I found it in a trunk in my attic." Gramz searches through her bedroom closet. "It was your mom's. Must have been a bridesmaid dress or something." She pulls out an emerald-green satin dress and spreads it out on her bed. "Can you believe I kept it all these years?"

The dress is sleeveless with a high neck. Tasteful black lace covers the bodice. Definitely a cool vintage look about it.

"It's beautiful, Gramz." I run my fingers over the soft fabric.

"Try it on." She unzips it.

I take off my T-shirt and hiking shorts and slip the dress over my head. I stand in front of the mirror. The dress is a bit big, but it still looks good on me. Really good. Brings out the blue-green of my eyes and looks great with my auburn hair.

"I thought you might want it. In case you haven't bought your graduation dress yet," Gramz says.

"You've been talking to Dad, haven't you?"

"Yes, and I agree with him. There is no reason you shouldn't go to your graduation."

"I can think of a few reasons."

Gramz stands behind me looking in the mirror. "See? Not too short and not too long. Just the right length to show off those fancy black high-heeled sandals you bought last year." She takes some pins from the top of her dresser and pulls at the slack fabric. "Just needs a bit of nip and tuck. Won't take me a minute to sew it up for you." She pins the fabric around both sides of the waistband.

"I don't even have a date for grad."

"So? Just go and have a good time with your friends. If I remember correctly, at Jeannie's graduation, she ended up dancing most of the night with a guy who wasn't even her date."

"Scandalous," I say and take another long look at myself in the mirror.

MOUNTAIN LOVE

When I drive up to the house, I see an SUV parked in front. It's nice and dirty, like it's been on a back road somewhere. So far so good.

I open the back door and hear a woman's voice and then Dad laughing. I can't remember the last time I heard Dad laugh like that.

"I'm home," I say as I drop my backpack and take off my hiking runners.

"Hey there." I walk into the kitchen to see Dad holding a glass of red wine. Now that's different. A slim and fit woman stands behind him. "Abby, I want you to meet Angela."

Angela puts down her glass of wine and walks toward me. She's wearing jeans and a white blouse. Her brown hair's cut in a stylish bob that almost touches her shoulders. "Hi Abby, so nice to meet you." Dad must have warned her about my face because there's only a tiny flinch when she looks right at me with her round brown eyes. She gives me a warm hug that I didn't see coming. "Your dad tells me you've been climbing today."

"No climbing, plans changed. Just went into Banff instead and walked with my grandma—my mom's mom." Not sure why I said that last bit. The words just tumbled out of my mouth. I obviously have a territory issue.

"What happened today?" Dad asks, looking concerned. "Is everything okay?"

"Yeah, weird day is all. I'll tell you about it later."

"I hope you like barbecued lamb," Angela says.

"I love it," I say.

"Good friends of mine in Water Valley are sheep farmers. Best lamb ever," Angela says. "And as organic as it gets. No steroids, grass-fed..."

"And they sing lullabies to the flock every night before bed," Dad says, making Angela laugh and put her hand on his arm. "And the lambs count sheep in their sleep." Dad laughs at his own silly joke.

"Can I help with dinner?" I ask.

"No, Angela and I have been slaving in the kitchen all afternoon." He gives her a look. *The* look. My Dad is absolutely, totally, and hopelessly smitten with this woman.

***

"So here I am chatting away—to myself it turns out," Angela says. Candles are burning down, flickering shadows on the empty bowls and plates on the dining room table. I can't remember the last time we ate dinner by candlelight. "When I finally look around, this guy is *way* behind me, leaning against a tree, sweating profusely and gasping for breath."

We all laugh.

"Even though in his profile he said he was an avid hiker?" I ask.

"Yeah, can you believe it?" Angela says then takes a drink of her herbal mint tea. "And this was on the flat walking trail by the Bow River."

"Okay, wait just a minute. You made me hike Ribbon Creek—ten long, steep miles—and this guy gets an easy stroll by the river?" Dad teases.

"I wanted to see what you were made of right off the bat," Angela says with a big smile. She brushes her hair off her face. "And I was definitely not disappointed."

"Glad to hear I met with your approval," Dad says.

"I got so tired of men pretending to be someone they aren't. It's so annoying," she says.

"Dad had a similar experience with one woman he met for coffee. She posted an old photo of herself."

"If honesty and trust are supposed to be the foundations of a relationship," Angela says, "those people are definitely starting off on the wrong foot."

Dad gives her a smoldering smile. I want to tell them to get a room, but I bite my tongue.

"Dad tells me you like to travel."

"I do. Travel is a huge part of my life. In fact, next week I'm off to China for a conference, but I'm tacking on a hiking trip to Mount Kailash in Tibet."

"I'm so jealous," I say. "I've only hiked in the Rockies."

"Believe me, Abby. After hiking all over, I still think the Rocky Mountain range is the most beautiful and has the best hiking in the entire world. You're so lucky you can see those mountains from your backyard."

"Yes, we are," I say. I avoided looking at those mountains for months, but now it's not so bad.

"How long will you be gone for again?" Dad asks Angela.

"About three weeks," she says. I can tell Dad's a bit choked.

***

Dad and I say good-bye to Angela at the door.

"Thanks for making dinner," I say to her. "You were right about the lamb. It was delicious. And your roasted-veggie dish was amazing."

"My pleasure, Abby. It was great to meet you."

"Hey, what about my salad?" Dad asks.

"Meh."

"I'm embarrassed for talking so much tonight," Angela says. "Next time I'm going to keep my mouth shut and I want to hear all about you and your favorite hikes."

"Your life is way more interesting than ours," I say.

"Speak for yourself," Dad says.

"The next dinner's on me," I say. "I make a mean mac and cheese, and Dad and I'll blab all night about our mountain adventures."

"Sounds great. I love mac and cheese!" Angela says. "Best comfort food ever."

"Right?" I say. Angela hugs me again. I could get used to this.

Dad wraps his big arms around Angela and stays in that embrace for an uncomfortably long time. At least uncomfortable for me. When he finally loosens his tight grip, he kisses her on the cheek. I'm pretty sure that if I wasn't right here that kiss would have been *way* hotter.

A weird concoction of emotions come over me in a wave, seeing Dad with this other woman he's clearly gaga over. It's been almost ten years since Mom died. I haven't seen him this happy in a very long while and it's time for him to move on. But even though I encouraged him, somehow it still feels too early for me.

***

"It looks amazing on you, Bean," Jeannie says as I model the green dress for her on FaceTime. I love the soft feel of the satin on my legs as the dress swishes. "Gramz made it fit perfectly."

Hands on hips, I ham it up, strut across my bedroom, pivot, strut back like a catwalk model. Like Serena, Grace, and I used to do when we photographed or videoed one another. Who was that person I used to be?

"Wish she had dug that dress out of her attic for my grad," Jeannie says. "I love vintage."

"It's awesomely retro, isn't it?"

"Can't wait to come home and go to the grad banquet with you."

"Only losers go to grad with their sister and father."

"I'm pretty sure Dad already bought the tickets, so you're not going to have much of a choice in the matter."

"I'll scalp them. Everyone's always looking for extra dinner and dance tickets."

"You're impossible."

I notice Jeannie has a thick ball of hair on top of her head. I pull my hair up, but I still don't have enough to put it in a knot. I let it down and it falls almost to my shoulders.

I look at myself in the mirror from all angles. "I do look good, don't I?"

"Yeah, yeah. We've already gushed about how gorgeous you look. Now tell me more about Angela."

"Well, she talked a lot. Mostly about her disastrous online dates and her world travels."

"But did she seem nice? Is she a good match for Dad?"

I shrug. "Nice enough, I guess."

"You don't seem too sure."

"It's not Angela. It's just weird seeing Dad so obviously smitten. He's all smiley, googly-eyed, and bubbly around her. Like a silly kid. So not the dad I'm used to."

"Yeah, I never thought about that. In theory it's great that Dad's met someone, but actually being there to witness it must be so strange."

"It's made me miss Mom lately." I start to choke up. "So weird, but in some ways Angela reminds me of her. Maybe that's what stirred things up for me."

"Aw, Bean…"

"I am happy for Dad, I really am. And he's hardly brought out the Scotch lately."

"That's a good thing."

"Yup," I say.

"Hey, sorry I'm going to miss your drama performance. Isn't it coming up soon?"

I check the calendar on my phone. "Oh my God. It's next Friday. Feels way too soon!" I start to feel stressed right out.

"Do you feel ready?"

"Yeah. No. Maybe. I've been such a head case lately."

Jeannie looks at her phone. "Sorry, Bean, I'm late for my chem study group."

"Aren't you in chemistry with Caleb?"

Jeannie's cheeks turn pink. "Yes, Caleb happens to be in my study group. And before you ask, yes, we're still dating. But most of our dates seem to be meeting up at the library to study."

"Oh, the library," I joke. "Sounds hot."

"Talk later?"

"Sure, bye J. Love you."

She blows a kiss and signs out. I want Jeannie here with me, wrapping her arms around me in one of her monster hugs.

I look at myself in the mirror. Imagine myself onstage, bright lights shining on me, performing my monologue in front of the whole school. The whole community. Next week. A nervous shiver comes over me.

INSIDE OUT

B io class is over. I pack up my books and see Liam waiting for me at the door.

"How was the climb on Saturday?" Liam asks and follows me down the hall.

"Didn't go."

"How come?"

"Another bear incident," I say. Liam stops suddenly, as if his runners were glued to the floor. "What the…?" Liam looks truly concerned, which makes me smile.

"Not me. Just had to give a tourist shit for feeding rice cakes to a bear in the ditch."

"Holy! Now that takes the cake, so to speak."

"Ha ha." I'm surprised when he follows me to the gym.

"You always did act like Ranger Rick when it came to stupid tourists," he says.

"So not true."

"Remember the time when that car full of yahoos threw their fast-food garbage out the window in the parking lot at Castle Junction?

You turned into a monster. I thought you were going to rip someone's head off."

"Couldn't help myself. There was a garbage can only a few feet
from where they were parked. Idiots."

"I would have gone with you, Abby. Climbing, I mean. It's just that
my mom hasn't had a day off in weeks, and I wanted her to get away
for the weekend."

"I get it. Penny works like a fiend." We arrive at the gym.

"Abby…" Liam studies my face, then looks right into my eyes. By
the look on his face, he doesn't seem to notice or care about my scars
and sunken face.

"Yeah?"

Liam shakes the words out of his mind. "Never mind, it's nothing.
See you around."

"See you." Liam turns around and walks back down the hallway to
the stairs. I'm *so* curious what his "nothing" is all about.

***

At lunchtime, Dax and Mason had left in Mason's truck—tires
screeching and rocks flying on their way out of the parking lot—in
an obvious move to skip drama class. Something to put into my non-
existent gratitude journal.

"You're up next for rehearsal, Zoe. Please introduce your monologue to the class," Mr. Owen says.

Zoe walks to the screen set up at the front of the class. She's wearing
faded jeans with the knees blown out and a T-shirt with red lettering
that says *Come to the Dark Side. We have cookies.* Her long, thin
ponytail has been dyed from purple to orange. "My monologue is

titled 'Inside Out.'" Zoe nods at Carter to turn on the projector aimed at the screen.

A montage of photos outside a gray concrete prison appears on the screen. "My father has been in prison in New Mexico since I was four years old. I've lied to people my whole life about why I don't live with him. Made up stories that he worked overseas, or was in the army. Too ashamed of the truth." A photo of a newspaper headline reads "Holdup at New Mexico Bank and Trust." Mug shots of her father. "My first prison visit was when I was five. My dad was sitting in a small green room, his hands and feet shackled. I burst into tears when I saw him. I ran up to hug him, but a guard with a snake tattoo on his bald head grabbed my dad and threw him behind a glass wall. Dad wasn't allowed to touch me or anyone, not even my mother. That was the last time I saw him. 'Touching' hands on either side of a thick layer of glass."

She goes on to talk about how hard life has been on her family, especially her mother and younger brother. How they moved to Canada to be close to her grandparents. Zoe ends it off: "Every time I hear about a prison riot, or a prisoner being beaten up and killed, I wonder if I'll ever see my father again. In his letters, he assures me he'll be out soon. But I'm nervous to know him outside of prison, outside of our letters. I'm worried that I may never be ready to know him as a free man. I've only ever known him as he is now—a man who can never really reach me."

Zoe gets a rousing round of applause from everyone, including Mr. Owen, including me. Her monologue is amazing, and it's clear she's put in a ton of work. I'll have some serious competition for the summer internship. *Shit.*

***

I lean up against Rusty, waiting for Grace in the parking lot. Simon and Olivia hold hands as they walk to Simon's Jeep. Simon sees me and waves with a big smile. I remember when Liam and I were first together, it was like I was living life floating a few feet above the ground. I wave at Simon, and a jealous pang hits me just below the ribs.

Grace comes as a Sticky Hive package today. Briar and Serena tag along, obviously wanting a ride home, too. Serena is even thinner than usual. Her cheekbones stick out sharply.

"Hey," Briar says.

"Mind driving Briar and me to my house?" Serena says. Grace mouths "Sorry."

"Sure, no worries," I say, even though I am worried I might not have enough gas to get myself home after taxiing everyone else around. Grace hops in the front seat, the other two in the back.

Horses and cows graze in fields on either side of the gravel road. I look in the rearview mirror. Both Briar and Serena have their eyes glued to their cell phones.

"Feeling okay, Serena?" I say.

"Why do you ask?" She keeps texting, her eyes don't leave her phone.

"Just that you're looking really skinny these days."

"Oh that. That's just to piss my mom off. She keeps sending me back to the seamstress to take in my grad dress. But the joke's on me because she basically told me I can never be too skinny."

"Your mom actually said that?" Grace says.

"Not in so many words, but she congratulated me for losing eight pounds and bragged about it to her friends."

"Wish I could drop eight pounds," Briar says.

Grace turns around to face them. "Stop the madness! Just stop it." Grace is almost yelling. "All this talk about being too fat and wanting to be skinny is driving me crazy. You two are beautiful—most girls would do anything to look even remotely as good as you. So why can't you both just be happy the way you are?"

I look over at Grace. She could have said you three. Not the beautiful part, but the "be happy the way you are" part. Makes me wonder if I'll ever be truly satisfied with myself. At least I've been a bit easier on myself when I look in the mirror. Even though it feels fake, squashing negative thoughts with positive ones has helped.

Briar stretches her body over to the front seat and plays with the radio until she finds a station that plays techno-pop.

"No way. That music will make me drive off the road," I say. Briar harrumphs and flops back onto her seat.

"I'll find something," Grace says and fiddles with the radio dial until she finds Avril Lavigne singing "Girlfriend."

"At least turn it up," Briar says.

I do and start singing at the top of my lungs. Grace joins me in singing how Avril doesn't like some guy's girlfriend. We look at each other and crack up for no particular reason.

"You bitches," Serena blurts out. I look in the rearview mirror and she's giving me a killer look.

"Whoa, where did that come from?" Grace says.

"Abby, what's going on with you and Liam?" Serena asks.

"Here we go…" Grace has obviously gotten an earful and didn't tell me.

"What are you talking about?" I ask, pulling into the upscale subdivision where Serena lives.

"Liam's been acting so strange around me ever since the bush party. Did you talk to him?"

"Yes, but—"

"What did you say to him? He stormed out of the party right after, so you must have said something to make him leave."

"I didn't say anything. Ask Liam why he left." No way I'm getting into this with her.

"Did you say something to Liam about me?"

"Of course not."

"Let me just come right out and ask you, Abby. Are you trying to steal my date for grad?" Serena asks. "Is this what it's all about?" She sucks in her already sunken cheeks.

"Geez, Serena," Grace says. Even Briar looks shocked. I pull up to Serena's house that looks like a small castle. No moat with alligators or a drawbridge, but it does have a large turret.

"I've got my own date for grad." I just don't tell her it's my dad. And my sister. Grace gives me a "what the…?" look but luckily keeps quiet.

"Liam won't answer my texts, phone calls, or Facebook messages. And when I talk to him at school about plans for grad night, he always changes the subject or walks away."

"Maybe because you always come on so strong. You never give guys any space," Grace says. "They probably feel smothered."

"Did Liam walk you to phys ed this afternoon?" Serena asks me.

"Yeah, but—"

Serena opens her door, gets out, and slams the door. Briar sheepishly follows. "Thanks for the ride." She closes the door, hesitates, then follows Serena.

"What was that all about?" I say.

"Tell me why I've been her friend the past four years," Grace says.

"You're asking me?" I say.

"Okay, tell me. Who is this mysterious grad date you've been keeping from me?" Grace looks at me all wide-eyed for a juicy explanation.

DANCING WITH THE BEAR

There's a lineup of cars ahead of us filling up the school parking lot for the drama performance.

"Wow, looks like the whole community's out tonight," Gramz says.

"Springbank really rallies behind the school programs," Dad says. "It's impressive."

A nervous, feeling in my chest comes in waves. We find an empty spot and park. I see a group of grade ten students wearing astronaut costumes walk through the parking lot. Obviously staging their short play tonight. They're like the warm-up band for our graduation performances. I see Zoe with her mom and brother head into the school. I wonder who will end up winning the summer internship. If I can't settle this nervous feeling, I'm so going to bomb.

I walk Dad and Gramz to the gym door.

"You're going to be amazing tonight," she says, holding my hand.

"Good luck, kiddo," Dad says. He first puts a hand on my shoulder and then wraps me in a hug. I'm shocked. And happy.

"Meet you here later," I say.

Before I lock my purse in my locker (yes, I now have a lock), I search the "Evolve" Facebook page on my phone, close my eyes, and scroll and scroll. I open my eyes and read this: "Whatever the present moment contains, accept it as if you had chosen it." *Hmm...*

I start down the hall toward the stairwell to head up to the drama room where all the performers are meeting.

"Hey, Abby," Carter says as he and Leon run to join me.

"You look nice," Leon says. I changed clothes about a hundred times. I started with my hiking shorts, boots, and backpack—sort of a lame costume—but ended up wearing the sundress I bought when I was shopping with Tammy.

"Thanks. How's it going?" I ask.

"To be honest I'm so nervous I could puke," Leon says.

"Join the party," I say. We start up the stairs.

"Remember when we were in like, grade three, no cares in the world, performing in front of an audience?" Carter says. "When did we get so insecure and self-conscious?"

"All I know is growing up sucks, big time," I say.

"You're so right about that," Leon says.

We get to the landing. Memories flash through my mind: Mason, Dax, and stoner posse; *Bear Bait*; poor Leon; the UR SO FN UGLY Messenger memes. I catch a glimpse of my reflection in the window. *Breathe deeply.*

***

"Listen up, people," Mr. Owen says to the performers in the drama room. "Best to just stay backstage, but if you have to leave for any reason, let Mrs. Schultz know. She will be keeping track of everyone."

I look around the room. Tali is on the verge of tears, Tammy's a bit nervous, Mason points his chin at me and Dax looks over, Leon and Carter are jumpy and play boxing, and Zoe is incredibly calm. Maybe she knows this is a slam-dunk for her.

"Questions? No?" Owen continues. "Okay, get out there and break a leg everyone."

When we gather backstage, I hear a rumble of voices in the gym. I open the stage curtains a crack and see that pretty much every chair is taken. Gramz and Dad are sitting close to the front. Serena, Briar, Keegan, Liam, and Gus are hanging out at the back. Grace, Simon, and Olivia have front-row seats. I remember feeling a bit uneasy before last year's performance when I was Joan of Arc, the lead performer. But that was nothing like the jitters I have tonight.

After the grade tens perform, it's Carter and Leon, Zoe, Tammy, and Mason and Dax. Then an intermission. I'm on right after the break. Tali's last.

Although I really want to watch the grade tens' *Star Trek* spoof, I have to pee. Again. "Just going to the washroom," I tell Schultzy, who is checking her clipboard.

"No lollygagging in there, Abby, okay?" she says.

***

As I wash my hands, I look at myself in the mirror. I packed on the makeup so thick it looks like a mask. At this very moment, I decide not to hide behind my makeup. I stare at myself for a long time then wet a paper towel and scrub off all the foundation and concealer caked on my face. My scars are now visible, my cheek looks even more sunken, and my wonky eye still doesn't open very wide. But this is me. The real me. As I am. I take the bear figurine out of my pocket, look at it closely, and hold it tightly in my hand. My talisman.

I lean against the door with my shoulder to open it, and Mason and Dax push me back into the bathroom. Mason locks the door behind him.

"What the…?" My heart starts to pound. The figurine drops out of my hand and lands on the floor.

"Nice! A souvenir," Dax says picking it up and stuffing it in his pocket.

"Give that back!" I yell.

Mason covers my head with a cloth bag, while Dax holds my arms behind me.

"Stop it!" I yell as loudly as I can, but it's muffled through the bag that smells like cigarette smoke and gasoline. It must be black because I can only see dim, muted light. I try to wriggle out of Dax's grasp, but I'm held even tighter. "Mason!"

I hear the tearing of tape, and then it's wrapped around my neck so the bag is secured in place. It feels tight. Constricting. My head is already hot, and I gasp for breath. Mason grabs my head with his big hands. "Told you I'd need a bag over your head, slut."

Dread floods my body. "You wouldn't."

Mason lets out a maniacal laugh, and it doesn't sound fake. "Definitely would—and will."

"Mason!" I yell. "Let me go. Please!"

"Shut the fuck up!" Mason says.

More tearing of tape. I wiggle and squirm to try to release from Dax's grasp. I'm terrified as my wrists and ankles get securely wrapped in duct tape.

"We gotta get out of here," Dax says.

My lump of a body is thrown forward, over a shoulder that I presume is Mason's. The click to unlock the door.

"Hallway's clear," Dax says.

I bump around as Mason runs down the hallway. I can hear Dax following. Down the stairs by the gym.

"Please, Mason. Let me go. Please!" I'm carried down another long hallway, and then I hear the clink of a key in a lock. A door opens. I'm flung down hard on the floor on my back, the door slams closed. It's dark, but I can tell by the stink of dirty rags and strong detergent that I'm in the custodian's closet. It's also quiet. Dax and Mason must have taken off to perform their stupid play. I fumble around and try to take the duct tape off my wrists. No way it's budging. I wriggle myself to a seated position and inchworm across the floor. I slam my head and shoulder against the door.

"Help! Please, help me! Someone!"

There's no one around this part of the school at this time of night. I pound my head and yell for a few more minutes before I give up. I start to feel sick from the smell of the bag and lack of air. And the adrenaline and terror. When I finally broke up with Mason, he told me that if he couldn't have me, he'd make sure no one else could. The thought of what he might do to me makes me shake uncontrollably, and it doesn't take long for the tears to race down my face.

I wonder what time it is. By now, Carter and Leon, Zoe, and maybe Tammy will have finished their performances. Mason and Dax would have made it back just in time. Schultzy is probably very pissed off with me for disappearing. I yell and pound my head one more time.

I do my best to chase out every thought of Mason that creeps into my mind. I think of the Evolve quote: "Whatever the present moment contains, accept it as if you had chosen it."

Well, my present moment of being hog-tied with duct tape and locked in a janitor's closet that smells of wet mops and detergent may be a wee bit hard to accept. Acceptance is definitely something I've struggled with this past year. And trust. Trusting that everything works out like it needs to. This is not a moment I would have chosen, but I clear my throat and begin to rehearse my monologue. I feel my hot breath as I speak into the bag covering my head. My voice—like my entire body—is shaky, but soon it sounds strong.

I have no idea how much time has passed when I finally hear footsteps and voices coming down the hall. "Help me!" Again I yell and pound on the door with my head. "I'm in here!" A key rattles the handle and the door pushes open.

"Oh my God!"

"Schultzy?" I say.

"You poor thing," she says and begins to unravel the tape around my neck. She pulls the bag off my head. Ms. Cooper, the custodian, swears under her breath, mumbles something about Mason stealing her key as she cuts the duct tape off my wrists.

"Are you all right?" Schultzy asks, her forehead folds in deep worried lines.

I shake my head, tears stream down my face. My wrists and ankles are finally free. I stand up on shaky legs and wipe away my tears. "Mason? Where is he?" I anxiously look up and down the hallway.

"He can't hurt you, Abby. And I'll do everything in my power to make sure he never comes near you again." Schultzy gently holds my arms. "We can talk about this later. But right now I'll get your father to take you home."

I slip out of her arms. "No way, Schultzy. I have to perform my monologue."

"After what you've just been through? No hon. I think it's best if you go home."

"I'm not going anywhere."

She gives me a concerned look. "Are you sure?"

I nod. "I *have* to do this."

"Then we'd better step on the gas. You're up next."

Ms. Cooper stays behind and locks up while Schultzy hurries me down the hallway. I see Mr. Hardy following Mason and Dax into his office. For the first time ever, Mason and Dax look scared shitless. I feel a strange mix of tremendous relief, fear, and…sorrow.

When we arrive backstage, everyone gives me a weird look, as if I tried to bail on the showcase. I can only imagine how I look after crying with a bag over my head for the past hour. I smooth down my hair, which is all tangled at the back.

Mr. Owen comes over, looking concerned. He knows something serious has happened, but he doesn't know what. "Are you sure you're up for this, Abby?"

I breathe deeply and nod. He puts his hand on my shoulder and gives it a gentle squeeze.

Schultzy peeks around the curtain. Tali is just finishing her monologue. This means I've been bumped to the very last performance of the evening. I cross my arms and hold them close to my body.

I hear the audience clap and whistle, and Tali bursts through the curtains looking pretty pumped. Mr. Owen walks through the curtains to the stage. I hear him say, "The last student from the graduating class is Abby Hughes, who will perform her monologue 'Dancing with the Bear.'" The audience claps. Owen peers at me through the crack in the curtains. Schultzy nods. I'm suddenly frozen in place. She takes me by the elbow and gives me a gentle nudge.

I walk through the curtains and onto the stage. The rumble of conversation dies down. A sea of faces stares at me. No one out there knows that I was just locked in a closet for almost an hour. Not even Gramz or Dad. My arms are still wrapped around me. I let go and try to stand tall. I put my hand in my pocket to hold the wooden bear but remember I dropped it in the bathroom. Dax has it. My whole body shudders for the audience to see. I look for Grace, who has a huge smile and gives me a double thumbs-up. Simon looks at me intently. He knows something's gone wrong. Although the stage lights are bright, I think I can make out Liam standing against the wall at the back of the gym. I slowly walk to the microphone and begin.

"The strange thing was I didn't feel anything, at least not while it was happening. Her bear smell was overpowering, like a hundred dead skunks on a pile of rotting leaves. I buried my hand in her thick, oily fur, maybe to push her away, I can't remember." My voice sounds weak and squeaky, my body is stiff. I take some deep breaths to relax.

"I looked into her small beady eyes, touched her nose, which reminded me of my dog Ruby's, black and wet. The bear was panting frantically. I heard a crunching and a slurping, realized it was my skull being crushed by her powerful jaw and sharp teeth. With my head in her mouth, I felt my body thrown around like a rag doll."

I desperately try to conjure up my performance memory as Owen taught us. I prepared well for this. "Your odds of being struck by lightning are one in three thousand. Drowning in a bathtub—one in eight hundred thousand. What's your chance of being mauled by a grizzly bear? Only one in two million. I always was one to beat the odds." Chuckles from the audience. This makes my tense shoulders loosen a little.

"It was last year, the weekend of June 20th. The day started out like every hiker's dream—a few fluffy white clouds floating in brilliant blue skies, and the sun felt especially warm. Five of us on a three-day backpack trip to Egypt Lake. Two of us had just completed grade eleven. The other three had all recently graduated and would soon be moving away to start new lives. This trip was really a final hurrah for them. The Parks Canada notice on the trailhead bulletin board read *Caution: grizzly bear sighted in the area.* We were a group of five crazies who had a habit of singing Abba songs at the top of our lungs while hiking." Laughs from the audience as I sing the chorus of *Mamma Mia* and dance around the stage. I'm starting to get into my body. Feel a rhythm. Next I sing a few lines from *Dancing Queen*. "No grizzly in its right mind would dare come near us." More laughs. I pause for a long moment to change the pace.

"My eyes were swollen shut. I could hear the hospital machines beep and hiss. Felt the rough skin of my dad's hand caressing mine. I touched my head. My hair was gone. I could only feel the zigzag of sutures and bandages, hardened with patches of dried blood. My grandma told me later that the only thing recognizable about me was my voice. For what felt like an eternity, I lived in a world inside my head, wondering if I was actually dead.

"Surgery number one: remove the dead scalp at the back of my head. Surgery number two: remove a drain that was syphoning fluids from my brain. Surgery number three: suture the pieces of my face back together. Surgery number four: take a skin graft from my thigh and apply it to the back of my head.

"It was our last day, we were hiking back down the trail to Healy Creek. I had to pee, so the others waited for me around a bend in the trail. I dropped my pack and went through some bushes, bent down to have a look at a purple wildflower I'd never seen before. I heard loud panting and a ferocious growl. I saw her two cubs first. Then a mass of brown fur charging me. My heart hammered in my chest as I scrambled up the nearest tree. Grizzlies may not be able to climb trees, but their six hundred pound bodies can barrel toward a tree as fast as thirty-miles an hour. I was sent flying. A horrific screeching came out of me that barely sounded human.

"Grizzly bears are a subspecies of the brown bear. Their life span in the wild is twenty to twenty-five years. Grizzly bears are top-of-the-food-chain predators, but most of their diet is made up of nuts, berries, fruit, bugs, leaves, and roots. Grizzlies dig dens, often in the side of hills, and hibernate for one hundred and fifty to two hundred and thirteen days. Females give birth while in hibernation and produce one to four cubs. Mothers are fiercely protective of their young, following their instincts—maternal, wild, and nurturing. I'm alive, and the mother grizzly bear is dead, shot by wildlife officers." I try to will the tears back into my head. My voice sounds shaky. "She was just trying to protect her babies. Rather than capture her cubs, wildlife officials decided to leave them in the wild, let nature take its course. One cub was hit by a train, the other was hit by a car." A few tears sneak down my cheeks. I wipe them with my hand.

"I touched what remained of my skull. It was an empty cavity. Warm blood oozing everywhere. I heard my friend screaming—I was terrified that the grizzly was going after him." I glance to the back of the gym at Liam. "I tried to call out his name but my mouth refused to work. I heard voices in the distance. Panicked voices. 'We'll go for help,' I heard. Someone covered me in sleeping bags. I drifted in and out of consciousness. The whoop-whoop-whoop of the helicopter woke me up.

"Surgery number five: remove the dead skin graft that didn't take. Surgery number six: a muscle from my back, the *latissimus dorsi*, is grafted to the back of my head. Surgery number seven: skin is grafted from my butt and placed on the back of my head. Yes, butthead is an appropriate name for me." Again, laughs from the audience. "My next surgery, number eight, will involve taking shavings of one of my ribs to build me a new cheekbone. This will kick off a series of even more surgeries.

"Month two in the hospital. After the bandages on my face were unraveled, I begged a nurse for a mirror. She reluctantly handed me one. When I first looked at my reflection, I told her the mirror was shattered, someone must have dropped it.

"This is my shattered face that I look at in the mirror every day—a patchwork of grafted skin and lines where the sutures were sown to hold my face back together. Every day I wish this didn't happen to me. I wake up each morning hoping it was just some bad dream. I tried to hide myself from the world for months, ashamed of my appearance and the scars on my body. The world outside my home reinforced my shame.

"Many people around the world believe that encounters with wild animals can give humans power, wisdom, and even good luck. I'm not sure about the good luck..." Soft chuckles from the audience. "...but my encounter with the grizzly has given me this: She has taught me that we all have 'bears' in our lives—an injury, an emotional scar, a disability, an insecurity, a grievance, an illness, an abuse. Some 'bears' are just more visible than others. For the past year, I've been running away and hiding from the bear in my life— from the fear, shame, and self-loathing. But I've come to understand she is part of me. She is my talisman.

211

"A wise woman once told me that I need to stop cowering and start dancing with my bear." I look at Gramz, who is wiping away a tear. "And I have to lead the dance. I can't let her stomp on my toes, swing me around too fast, or change the dance steps.

"To quote the Nigerian author Ijeoma Umebinyuo, 'Start now. Start where you are. Start with fear. Start with pain. Start with doubt. Start with hands shaking. Start with voice trembling but start. Start and don't stop. Start where you are, with what you have. Just...start.'"

I pause, and the audience begins clapping, cheering, and whistling. Grace, Simon, and Olivia jump to their feet for a standing ovation. Dad and Gramz are already standing. I look around for Liam, but he's gone. Was my monologue too painful for him? I bow and head through the curtains to backstage.

Schultzy is there, waiting for me with her arms wide open. I lean into her round, soft body and sob my heart out.

FACING THE MUSIC

Gramz's arm is wrapped around me as we walk with Schultzy to the office.

"How did you find me, Schultzy?" I ask.

"When you didn't show up backstage, I looked all over for you. Wondered if you'd just gone home," Schultzy says.

A police officer escorts Mason and Dax down the hall to the parking-lot exit. Through the office window I see Dad, Liam, and Mr. Hardy speaking with a second police officer.

"Liam?" I ask Schultzy. "What's he doing in there?"

"He is your true rescuer. He came backstage to wish you luck, and you were nowhere to be found. Then he overheard Mason and Dax boasting about what they'd done to you and saw them tossing this around." Schultzy digs into her sweater pocket and hands me my bear carving. "Apparently, he confronted them and there was quite a scuffle. Mr. Hardy had to break it up."

So that's why he left before the end. He needed to talk to the police. I hold the figurine tightly in my hand.

"I'm horrified you had to go through this, Abby, but because things escalated, there are now solid grounds for the police to deal with these boys," Schultzy says. "I have a strong feeling you haven't been their only target."

"What's going to happen to Mason and Dax?" I ask.

"As you can see, they've been arrested. The police will likely charge them with forcible confinement or maybe even kidnapping."

"That means there will be a trial and I'll have to testify."

"Maybe," Schultzy says, "but that's a long way off. They'll likely be held at a corrections facility for quite some time."

Through the office window, I see Liam talking as the police officer writes notes. Dad listens with a grave expression. When they are done, Schultzy knocks on the office door.

***

"I'll kick their scumbag, jerk-faced, snot-bucket, low-life asses!" Simon paces around my bedroom, punching a fist into his other hand. "Worthless bags of beaver crap!"

"Beaver crap?" I fall back on my bed laughing, my head landing on my soft pillow. It feels so good to laugh for a change.

"I should have been onto them, Abby." Simon sits on my bed.

"How would you, or anyone else for that matter, know what they were up to?"

"I knew what they were capable of."

"You're cute when you care so much." I pinch Simon's stubbly cheek and he blushes.

"Sorry I haven't been all that available lately," says Simon.

"Love will do that to a person."

"It's not love. Just serious like."

"Remember when Liam and I got together? I kind of dumped you for a while. That is, until I missed our crazy conversations, marathon movie binges, and gourmet gelato way too much."

Simon gets quiet. Looks down at his hands. "Olivia got into MIT."

"What's that?"

He gives me a look like I'm a total imbecile. "Massachusetts Institute of Technology? Ever heard of it? Only the top engineering university in all of the U.S., maybe even the world."

"Ontario isn't that far from Massachusetts, is it? Maybe you'll be able to meet up halfway."

Simon shakes his head. "In just three months everything's going to be so new and different."

"For you, maybe. Everybody's moving on with their lives. Everybody but me, that is. I get to spend a big chunk of my gap year either in the hospital or at home recovering from surgery. Same old, same old. *And* repeat."

Simon gets a text. "It's Olivia. She's on her way to my place."

"Is tonight the big night, if you know what I mean?" I raise my eyebrows up and down.

"We've already had sex, Abby. Lots of times."

"What?! And you didn't tell me?"

"It was none of your business."

"Well, so, what was it like?"

"I repeat. None of your business." Simon leans over and gives me a quick, stiff hug. "See you at the grad ceremony in the morning?"

"Yup."

"What about the banquet tomorrow night?"

"My dad said he'll disown me if I don't go."

"Good for Derek. Save me a dance?"

"You and dance in the same sentence?"

"Ha ha, very funny." Simon leaves.

I roll onto my back and stare at the crisscrossing veins of old plaster on my ceiling, pretending one of them is a road that will lead me to where I need to go.

***

That night, I dream that I'm waiting at the gate of a busy airport. My graduating class is all lined up—Grace, Serena, Simon, Briar, Liam, Tammy, Carter, Leon, and everyone else—waiting to board a flight. Officials are at the desk, checking passports and boarding passes, ushering people aboard the flight. I join the line, hold tightly to my boarding pass. When I finally get to the desk, the airline agent tries to scan my boarding pass, but it's blank. It won't scan. I keep asking her to try again and again. I'm directed to get out of the line so others can board the flight.

AND THE WINNER IS...

For the morning graduation ceremony at Calgary's Jube, formally known as the Southern Alberta Jubilee Auditorium, Dad and Gramz stand at the back while I walk across the stage in my cap and gown. As Mr. Hardy hands me my high school diploma rolled up with a red ribbon, both wave enthusiastically. Gramz blows me a kiss. They have to leave right now so she can catch her flight to Bali. Dad will drop her off at the airport and pick up Jeannie.

The graduating class is seated in alphabetical order. Grace Chelanga is in the second row, Briar Edwards is in the next row. Serena Halstead is at the end of my row. Leon Labelle and Carter Lee are right behind me. Liam Thompson and Simon Williamson are several rows behind. No Dax Brozik. No Mason Jamieson.

I'm almost crushing my graduation diploma as I wait for the endless awards to be handed out. Awards for the outstanding athletes, best sportsmanship, citizenship, academic recognition in every subject area, most improved student, best volunteer, outstanding junior musician, and outstanding senior musician. When I see Mr. Owen head to the microphone, I know he's going to announce the award I've been waiting for. My heart pounds so hard I can feel my ears heat up.

"The winner of this next award, for the best performance at our Graduate Drama Showcase, will also be invited to attend a summer workshop with Theater on the Edge. I'd like to invite Mike Storm and Denise McSweeny, artistic directors of Theater on the Edge, to present the award."

A man and a woman seated onstage stand and walk to the microphone.

Denise talks first. "I just want to say what an honor it was to attend Rocky View High School's Graduate Drama Showcase last week. I have to tell you, both Mike and I were blown away by the talent in your school's drama department."

"After having the privilege of experiencing such powerful performances, it was a very difficult decision to choose just one student. But after much deliberation," Mike says, "the winner of the Theater on the Edge summer internship for her monologue performance is…Zoe McMaster for 'Inside Out.'"

My heart does a flip-flop. Everyone cheers as Zoe heads to the stage for her award and has her photo taken with Mike and Denise. I finally start clapping. If Zoe performed at the showcase even half as well as she did in rehearsal, she deserves this. Big time.

Mike and Denise return the microphone. Mike says, "As we said earlier, this was not an easy decision. Two of the performances stood out for us, and it was difficult choosing a clear winner. Therefore, Theater on the Edge has decided to also invite Abby Hughes to perform her monologue, 'Dancing with the Bear,' at our summer festival. Abby, could you please stand up."

I'm in shock. I slowly stand. People clap and cheer. Runner-up is still pretty sweet.

"Please give a big round of applause for all the graduates of the drama department," says Mr. Owen. "It has been an honor to be your teacher over the past four years." I clap and look around at my fellow drama students, including Tammy, Carter, Leon, Tali, and Zoe. Mr. Owen bows as the drama class gives him a standing ovation.

***

Everyone is milling about in the foyer of the auditorium. I look around but don't see Liam. Serena, Briar, and Grace are huddled in a corner. Grace shakes her head, walks toward me rolling her eyes.

"Want to get pissed this afternoon?" Grace asks.

"Are you nuts?"

"That's what Serena and Briar are planning on doing. Serena stole some booze from her mom, and they're going to start drinking before the banquet."

"So not a good idea," I say.

"That's what I told them, but they're not listening."

"Anyone else joining them?"

"No. Justin, Liam, Briar, Keegan, and I are meeting at Serena's for photos, then going to the convention center from there."

"In a limo?" I ask, feeling like the biggest loser ever, especially as I'll be going with Jeannie and Dad in the truck.

"Yeah, Serena's mom is bucking up for it. How could her little, drunk girl go to grad in just any ol' vehicle?"

A pang of jealousy hits me hard. I always imagined Liam and me going to grad together in a limo.

"Need a ride home?" I ask.

"No, thanks. I probably should go home with my mom." Grace looks into the crowd of people. "She's here somewhere."

"See you tonight, Grace," I say.

"I'm so proud of you, Abbs." Grace gives me a big hug. "Performing in the summer festival is such an honor. Shit, did I just sound like somebody's mother?"

"Yeah, but I could use a mother right about now." Grace kisses me on the cheek.

Outside the auditorium, everyone is having photos taken with their families, selfies with their friends. Everyone looks so excited to be moving on with their lives. All I feel is empty and alone, like I'm being left so far behind. With a blank boarding pass.

I walk to my car and get in. Take my cell phone out of my purse, search the Evolve page, close my eyes, and scroll. "If your life isn't going the way you want, it's time to start hanging out with your future and stop hanging out with your past."

I watch Tammy and her mom getting their photo taken. Tammy, who has gone through—and is still going through—way more than me, looks so proud, so confident, so hopeful for her future. Determined to live that authentic life that she talked about in her monologue, even with all the struggles she faces. Makes me wonder: if I'd strutted into my new life the way Tammy did, instead of hiding at home for months, maybe I'd be farther ahead in the self-acceptance department. *Hey world, here I am. Whether you're ready for the new me or not.* I turn the rearview mirror toward me and look closely at my face. I smile my weird, wonderful, crooked smile. And for the first time in a very long while, I can see the real me reflecting back. I like what I see.

I search the contacts on my phone. "Hello, this is Abby Hughes. I'm calling to cancel my surgery with Dr. Van der Meer scheduled for eight o'clock on the morning of July 17 at the Foothills Hospital. No, I won't be rescheduling the surgery. No, I don't need to make another appointment. Thanks, good-bye."

I search the Internet for a number and dial it. "Hi, may I please speak with someone about applying to the Faculty of Education. Yes, for this September."

***

"Oh my God, Bean! Huge life decisions you made, and all in one day," says Jeannie, laying out eye shadow, lipstick, and makeup brushes on the bathroom counter. She's already dressed for the banquet in a short black sleeveless dress. "What do you think Dad will say about you canceling your surgery?"

"He'll be shocked and give me the are-you-sure-this-is-the-right-course-of-action speech, but I think he'll understand that I want to just get on with my life." I look at myself in the mirror. "Besides, he's always told me that it's my decision whether or not I have more surgery."

"Do you think you might change your mind?"

I shrug. "Not sure. But right now I want to try life just the way I am and see what happens."

Jeannie wraps me in a hug so tight it feels like my ribs might break.

"I've missed you more than the smell of Dad's stinky work socks, Bean," she says.

"I've missed you more than the green fuzz on expired yogurt."

"I've missed you more than Ruby's barf after she's eaten a dead rodent."

We both crack up. "Ah, nice one, J."

Jeannie, my makeup coach, looks at me like an artist observing her canvas. I'm already wearing mascara, and the concealer has lived up to its promise to last all day.

"You need way more of the green eye shadow on your eyelid and then the brown in the crease. You've got to show off your beautiful eyes." She sticks a makeup brush into a container of emerald-green eye shadow.

"I'll look like a hooker."

"Close your eyes and trust me."

I do as I'm told. The brush tickles my left eyelid. I can barely feel the right one because of the scarring.

"When it comes to makeup, more is more on grad night. Everybody will want to take selfies with you."

"We'll see about that." I stop myself. Switch it around. "Yes, everyone will be taking selfies with me because I am going to look absolutely stunning." At least Grace and Simon will want to.

"Open your eyes."

The eye makeup is way more than I have ever worn in my entire life, but I will trust Jeannie on this one.

Jeannie picks up a tube of lipstick. "Now you need a more subtle color on your lips. This one's called Stepping Out. Perfect." Jeannie giggles as I roll my eyes.

She paints my lips with the pinkish-brown shade.

"Now let's see the hair," Jeannie says. "Good job blow-drying, but I thought Dad was going to spring for a hairstylist."

"I told him to save his money. Besides, the bald patches have mostly grown in."

"Now put on the dress," Jeannie says, squealing with excitement.

I take off my skirt and blouse, slip on the satiny green dress, and stand in front of my full-length mirror. I almost don't recognize myself.

Jeannie gasps and puts her hand over her mouth. "Oh, Bean…"

The old Abby would have translated Jeannie's gasp as being horrified at how ghastly I look. But I know she thinks I look amazing, and I have to agree with her. My scars, crooked smile, and all.

DON'T YOU (FORGET ABOUT ME)

The grad banquet is held in downtown Calgary at the convention center. A big deal. I wait at the entrance while Dad and Jeannie park the truck. Limo after limo line up and out come my fellow graduates, looking so handsome and beautiful. Tammy and her date, Charley. Leon with a girl I don't know. I realize that after I write my last final exam, I may never see many of these people again. I feel kind of sad.

An enormous white limo pulls up. Justin, looking awkward in his dark-brown suit and tie, gets out and holds out a gentlemanly hand for Grace. She looks radiant in a long, silvery off-the-shoulder dress. She runs up to me, her high heels clicking on the pavement.

"Oh my God, Abbs, you look amazing."

"You, too. I knew that dress would look gorgeous on you."

"Please save me from the Serena madness," Grace says as Briar, Keegan, and Serena spill out of the limo. "She's already slurring her words."

Serena looks more like a bride in her white lacy sleeveless gown. Her bony shoulders and collarbones stick out sharply.

"Where's Liam?" I ask.

"When he got to Serena's and saw how drunk she was, he bailed. Said he'd drive himself. Didn't even stay for pictures."

Does this niggling feeling in my stomach mean I'm glad? Relieved? Pissed off? All of the above?

"Can't imagine that went over well."

"Like you'd expect. She hurled every insulting name at him she could think of and then poured herself another stiff one."

Serena stumbles but grabs Briar's arm to steady herself, and they wobble into the convention center. Justin stands at the door waiting for Grace.

"I'd better get going. See you in there." Grace hugs me then joins Justin.

As they walk toward me, Jeannie's chatting away with Dad, catching him up on all her news.

"Shall we?" I say.

"We certainly shall, Gorgeous," Jeannie says.

A wave of pure joy washes over me as the three of us link arms and make our way to the door. The dining room is packed with about a hundred tables. With a sudden self-preservation reflex, I look around for Mason and Dax, even though I know they are in police custody. Fine by me.

Simon and Olivia, their eyes glued to each other, are at a table with Simon's dad, Olivia's parents, and Gus and his parents. Simon gives me a smile and a thumbs-up. Grace and Justin are sitting at a table with Justin's parents and Grace's mom and her new man, who's wearing a loud plaid suit. Grace looks bored stiff. Briar, Keegan, and Serena are at a big table with their parents. Briar and Serena are joined at the forehead, laughing like hyenas. Serena's mother, who usually is very elegant and composed, has an annoyed expression. Serena's dad talks on his cell phone.

Liam and Penny sit at a table with a strange mix of students from the beekeeping club, the anime club, and the ping-pong club. With her dyed reddish-pink hair, Penny looks so out of place among this crowd of mostly Nordstrom mothers. She spots us, gets Dad's attention, and points out the three empty chairs beside them. Dad nods and leads us to the table.

Oh, great.

When Liam sees me, his eyes widen. I wish I could read his face, but I'm going to assume he likes what he sees. He stands, shakes Dad's hand, and gives Jeannie a quick wave. Then he stares at the swirly pattern on the carpet.

Penny hugs me. "You look absolutely smashing, Abby."

"Thanks, Penny."

Dad pulls out chairs for Jeannie and me, but I'm too antsy. I need the murky air cleared before I can enjoy the evening.

"Liam, can I talk to you?" I say.

He nods, reluctantly follows me out of the dining room into the foyer.

"What the hell?" I say.

"What?" He has the audacity to look surprised.

"You dumped me months ago when I needed you the most."

"I know, I thought we'd already established that I'm an asshole." He's super-agitated, but I'm on a roll.

"And you promised me over a year ago we would go to grad together no matter what. Do you know that one of the only reasons I came back to Rocky View High was to go to grad with you?"

"I'm sorry, but—"

"Not only that, but then you agreed to go to grad with Serena and bailed on her at the last minute. How do you think she feels?"

"I should never have said yes to Serena in the first place. Look, Abby...I didn't think you'd ever want to go to grad with me—the chickenshit loser."

"You stood up to Mason and Dax. Hardly what I would call a chickenshit loser."

"I was worried about you," Liam says softly, hanging his head.

I sigh and take in how hot he looks in his navy suit and striped tie.

"If only you'd talked to me," I say.

"I couldn't." Tears well in his eyes and his lower lip starts to quiver. "I just couldn't."

I want to hold on to my rage, my righteous indignation, but instead a warm tsunami of compassion floods my whole body. I wrap my arms around Liam and we hold each other for what seems like hours before we finally go back to the table.

***

Dinner's over. While Jeannie talks to Schultzy and Mr. Hardy, I dance with Dad.

"Glad you came tonight?" Dad asks.

"Yeah, I am. Thanks for threatening to disown me if I didn't come."

"I threatened to disinherit you—I'd never disown you."

"Well, thanks for that." Dad gives me a big hug. It feels so good. Must be getting lessons from Angela. Speaking of...

"What's new from Angela the environmentalist?" I ask.

Dad smiles. "She texted a few times from China. I'm still on her radar."

"Sounds promising."

"That it does."

"You deserve to be happy, Dad."

"So do you, Abby. So do you." Another warm hug.

***

After dancing with Dad, I go to the washroom. Grace and Briar are standing outside a stall.

"What's going on?" I ask, then hear puking sounds.

"Serena's had a little too much to drink tonight. Apparently, she was slipping booze into her punch during dinner," Grace says. "Briar, go get Serena's mom. Serena needs to get home to bed."

"No way, her mom will kill her. Besides, Serena's been talking about the after-grad party for the whole year," Briar says.

More puking. Moaning.

"I don't think Serena's going to any after-grad party tonight," Grace says.

Briar hesitates then leaves. I look under the stall and see that Serena's white dress is stained with barf. "You okay in there?" I ask.

Serena says something incoherent and pukes again.

After Serena's parents take her home, I go back to the table where Liam, Penny, Jeannie, and Dad are talking. The music starts again and Liam stands, holds out his hand to me.

The song is "Don't You (Forget About Me)" by Simple Minds. We dance. Dance like we used to, all crazy-like. Shaking our bodies, twisting, twirling each other around, and laughing our asses off like no one else in the world exists.

ACKNOWLEDGEMENTS

Oceans of thanks go to:

Diana Cranstoun, Tricia Dower, Adrian Hill, Diana Jones, and Shannon McFerran—my insightful and talented writing friends, whose thoughtful comments on those raw early drafts nudged me to finish this novel.

Susan Mayse who has challenged me to deep dive into the art and craft of writing and offered much needed encouragement along the way.

Becca Lee and Ijeoma Umebinyuo for allowing me to use their beautiful words.

Heather Camlot who helped shape the story with her remarkable editing prowess.

Kathryn Cole who uncovered the story's potential, and the entire team at Second Story Press.

My family and friends who have been my most devoted cheerleaders, even when I didn't think there was much to cheer about.

ABOUT THE AUTHOR

Born in Calgary, Alberta, Leanne Baugh first fell in love with writing for film. She won three screenwriting awards and had two screenplays optioned. She soon switched to writing fiction and recently finished her third Young Adult novel. When she isn't at home walking the beaches in Victoria, B.C., she's off travelling the world.